They Came To Riba

JOHN DYSON

A Black Horse Western

ROBERT HALE · LONDON

ISBN 0 7090 6751 8

Robert Hale Limited
Clerkenwell House
Clerkenwell Green
London EC1R 0HT

Typeset by
Derek Doyle & Associates, Liverpool.
Printed and bound in Great Britain by
Antony Rowe Limited, Wiltshire.

They Came To Riba

JayCee Lanchester, the richest rancher in Arizona's Tonto Basin, runs the town of Riba, keeping his daughter Margarita a virtual prisoner. But Margarita's chance meeting with lanky Welsh-Texan Cal Jones spells love at first sight for the two young people, and a bitter cordial for her father. Not only is Jones a sheepman, but he has flouted rules to bring his drought-thirsty flock down from the Mogollon Rim to the water hole in the basin.

With a whole valley soon feuding and fighting, the two young lovers are torn apart by ignorance and hatred. To make matters worse, evil Jake Houck and his gang arrive in Riba to hunt down Jones. After gunning down JayCee and kidnapping Margarita, Houck and his gang use her to lure the peace-loving Jones into an ambush.

Alone, and with only six bullets left, what chance in hell does he have of rescuing her?

One

'Maybe we made the wrong decision going into sheep.' Old-timer Randy Newbolt scratched at his grey thatch and contemplated the dried jigsaw cracks of mud that had once been their waterhole. 'Maybe we shoulda stuck with cows.'

His young partner, Cal Jones, sucked on a pebble for the saliva it stimulated in his dry mouth. He pulled off his Stetson, wiped the sweat from his brow and scraped back his long, flaxen hair. 'You say Indian Wells hole is dry, too?'

'All but – it will be if we don't get rain within a week or two.' Randy squinted up at the clear blue Arizona sky. 'And there ain't much hope of that.'

The six-foot Texan strolled across to the sheer cliff edge of the high mountain range known as the Mogollon Rim and looked down at the pale greens and ochres of grass and trees, rocks and stream beds hazing away into the distance of the Tonto Basin. At that height, the fierce breeze flapped the torn leather batwing chaps against

his long legs and worn high-heeled boots, flut-
tered the 'stars and bars' bandanna about his
throat. He turned and studied the scraggy bunch
of sheep, about 500 head, some of which were
plaintively nuzzling at the dried mud. 'These critters need water same as any others. We're gonna
have to take 'em down,' he said.

'That ain't a good idea, Cal, an' you know it.'
Randy spoke in a hoarse, high-pitched, old man's
voice. 'Those are cow men down there and you
know what they think of sheep. You want a war,
you'll get it.'

The young man thoughtfully rolled the brim of
his tall-crowned hat into a more pleasing shape
and crammed it on his head. He spat out the
pebble and drawled, 'Maybe I can talk them into
seein' sense. It's a free range this end of the valley
and there's enough water for everybody. I ain't
gonna just blunder in. I'll go down first, speak to
the Tilburys, ask their permission.'

'Son, if you don't mind me saying, your mama
musta dropped you on your head. Or you're just
plain naive. Where you think they're gonna tell
you to go? To the fiery inferno, thass where.'

'Maybe I'm hoping they'll have the decency to
see we've got no alternative. There's plenty of
room for us down there if we keep to the lower
slopes. Maybe if I explain to them that the sheep
won't hurt their cattle—'

'They'll welcome you with open arms? Boy, you
must be joking.'

Cal went over to his mustang which, like the sheep, was trying to get moisture by nibbling on a thorn bush. He collected the reins and swung into the saddle. 'It's worth a try.'

'I musta needed my head examining when I let you talk me into this venture,' Randy wheezed, as he went over and climbed onto his own horse. 'I shoulda stayed in Tucson and opened a store.'

'There's good money in sheep. More than in tough old longhorns.'

'Yep, but longhorns are tough enough to survive this drought. Even if we could nurse our babies through it, look at the state of 'em. What kind of price are walkin' skeletons goin' to make at market?'

'Try to look on the bright side, Randy, you old misery-guts,' Cal smiled, as they walked the broncs back to their corral and lean-to. 'Where are the boys?'

'Where you think? Out looking after our investment. That's another puzzle to me: how we ever gonna pay their back wages?'

'We'll find a way, don't worry.'

'What if the Tilburys tell you to get lost?'

'Then maybe I'll just have to ignore their advice.'

'That would be inadvisable, Cal, and you know it.'

They had employed four Tonto Apaches to shepherd their flock, splitting their 2,000 sheep into groups and moving them along the bleak plateau of the mountain range, finding grazing where they could. Unlike the fierce Chiracahuas, Cochise and Geronimo and their band, the Tonto had been pacified a long time and tried to adapt to the ways of the white men who had taken over their land.

'Sounds like one of the chooks has provided breakfast,' Cal said, as he heard a victorious cackling coming from their makeshift henhouse. He ducked inside, removed a warm egg from beneath the red-chopped fowl, and found three more in another nest. 'Thanks. ladies.'

He filled the chickens' water bowl from the last of the brackish supply in their barrel, and went into the shade of the rock lean-to built up inside a hollow of the cliff, roofed with pine boughs. He poked up the fire in their iron stove and fried two of the eggs in oil, tipping them out onto a tin plate for his pard. He ate his own straight from the pan, washing them down with thick black coffee, sitting on a wooden mule saddle for lack of any chair, or table, or other home comforts.

'It's the Fourth of July tomorrow,' Randy said, as he removed his set of false teeth after eating, and carefully replaced them in his vest pocket. 'They'll be having a shindig down in Duppa Springs. If you're going down into the valley, while you're there you might as well go enjoy yourself. We could do with some coffee, flour, beans, and a few bits and bobs.'

'You comin', too?'

'Nah, I'll stay here. My days of rodeoing and dancin' are over, but young feller like you needs to root, hoot and holler now an' again. You're far too serious for your own good.'

'Well, you ain't exactly a li'l ray of sunshine, yourself,' Cal grinned, as he went to clean the plates in the dust.

'What a young feller like you wants to hide himself away up in these hills fer, I'll never know. I figure it's high time you got yourself a wife, give you somethang to do with your nights. Hey, while you're there why doncha wed one of them cute li'l Mex *tamales*? She could make herself useful doing the cooking and washing and whatnot.'

Cal listened to Randy gabbling on, gummily, and said, 'Waal, I guess I could try ta raise some cash at the hoss races. But I cain't see even a li'l Mex *tamale* wanting to be the unpaid domestic for you and me.'

'Aw, you're a handsome enough young feller, you could talk her into it.'

'Randy, doncha think we got enough troubles without wanting another mouth to feed, and, who knows, maybe more mouths after that? If I ever think of gettin' hitched it'll be when I've got enough money in the bank to live decent. And I won't just be lookin' for a bedwarmer, cook and laundry maid. I've allus figured I'd prefer to pair up with a gal whose spirit and mind I respect, more of a soulmate. It's a long time you're thrown together.'

'You're optimistic, aincha? In this country, gals is few and far between. You gotta git what you can git.'

'Waal, maybe I *will* take a shave 'fore I head to town,' Cal smiled. 'You never know, do ya?'

He didn't wear a sidearm like most men in those parts; he always figured it was asking for trouble. He had been brought up by God-fearing folks and he was a man of peace by nature. But he did carry a long-range Creedmore, solid iron-frame rifle tucked back in its saddle holster beneath one leg as he carefully manoeuvred his mustang, Mosquito – so-called because he was a pain in the butt – down the steep sheeptrail into the valley.

There was good reason why this end of the basin was free range, unclaimed land. It was rocky and cut through with treacherous ravines, with thin patches of grass and poorly watered. There were tall clumps of rock, miniature mountains, infested with cactus thorn in which the last of the mountain lions and black jaguar made their lairs, venturing out to prey on lambs and calves. That was why he carried the rifle. A man never knew when he might come face to face with one. Such creatures were not averse to attacking humans.

Once past Duppa Springs in the centre of the valley, the Basin widened out into areas of lush gramma grass which had, naturally, been claimed by the early frontiersmen who tamed the Apache.

Latecomers to this part of the territory, like the Tilburys and Cal Jones himself, had to make what they could of this unclaimed rough wilderness on the northern slopes of the Basin.

The Tilburys were rough and ready Missouri drifters who had settled at this spot and made a sparse living running longhorns. The shacks they had raised as house and barns had not many more comforts than Cal's lean-to, but they did have a well and access for the cattle to a water-hole.

It was nearly high noon when the Texan spied the windmill of their water pump and the mercury was well up over the 100°F mark, a dry, dull heat that rasped the breath in a man's lungs.

Suddenly, a rifle shot rang out, spurting the dust beneath his mustang's feet and ricocheting away. Cal hung onto his reins trying to calm his prancing horse and caught the gleam of sunlight on a gunbarrel up in a heap of rocks. Another shot whined past his cheek, nearly taking off his earlobe.

Cal raised his arm, hand out-stretched in the peace sign, and shouted, 'Hold it! I'm here to talk.'

'Clear off, sheepman,' a youth's voice yelled from the rocks. 'We ain't got nuthin' to talk about. I'll count to ten and then I'll start shootin' for real.'

'Hold on! I just want to talk to your father, friendly-like.' Cal wondered if he stayed where he was the boy, Noah, would carry out his threat. He seemed a tad demented. 'Look, I ain't got no side-arm.'

'That's your bad luck, mister.' But it must have reassured the youth because he showed himself, hillbilly-ish in floppy hat, filthy wool vest and baggy trousers. 'How about that rifle in the boot?'

Cal raised his arms. 'Come and take it and follow me in.'

'Huh?' Noah Tilbury eyed him, dubiously, from his vantage point. 'Maybe I'll just do that. You keep grabbing air, mister. Don't try no funny tricks.'

'I ain't here for funny tricks. I'm just here to speak to your old man.'

'Yeah, what you damn well want?' Noah climbed down, his boots as busted and sun-bleached as Cal's. 'Hmm?' he muttered, sliding out the Creedmore. 'Not a bad piece.' He tossed it away into the scrub and growled, 'Now you jest ride in slowly, keepin' them hands high.'

'Jeez!' Cal raised his eyes to the heavens, shook his head, and nudged his bronc forward with his knees. 'You're real neighbourly, aincha?'

The old man, Blade Tilbury, was even more runtish and sour-faced than his son. He came out of his wooden shack with a shotgun in his hands, followed by his scrawny wife. Her face was weather and work-beaten, and her dress shabby.

'Yuh, sheepman, what you want?'

'It's like this, the drought's giving us hard times up on the Rim. If we don't get our animals to water we're gonna be wiped out. I want your permission to bring them across your land.'

'Git lost.'

'Look, we're not gonna graze your grass. We'll keep 'em up on the sides of the Rim. We just need access to your waterhole. . . .' But, however hard he tried to explain, he was met with mute incomprehension, or a monosyllabic, 'Go to hell.'

The woman tried to intervene. 'He seems a decent young fella. Surely we could let him just this once?'

Tilbury told her, curtly, 'Shut up. Go poke your nose someplace else. Once would lead to twice an' then he'd have proven rights. There ain't gonna be no once, not fer vermin like sheep.'

The wife shrugged and rubbed her hands in her apron. 'Well, at least let him water his horse at the trough.'

'No, he ain't gonna do that, neither. We ain't got no free water for sheepmen scum. Let me give you fair warning, mister: if I see your animals anywhere near our waterhole I'm gonna start shootin'. Jest fergit it. Now, you've said your piece, so clear off my property. I don't want to see hide nor hair of you again.'

'Yeah, thass right,' Noah yelled. 'Go on. Git.' And he fired his rifle at the horse's hooves, too close for comfort this time. Mosquito was kicking and dancing and snorting his annoyance.

Cal grabbed the reins as the bullets spurted up dust, and he hauled the mustang around, steadied his hand, and started off back down the trail, pausing only to retrieve his Creedmore.

'Aw, well,' he said, patting his horse's neck. 'I guess we'll go take a look at the rodeo.'

TWO

The hoe-down at Duppa Springs to celebrate the Fourth of July was in full swing as the moon rose high. Lusty ranch hands up on the raised platform whooped and kicked spurred boots as they danced back and forth and swirled rosy-faced farm wenches. Fiddles were scraping, tambourines trembling, a medicine drum pounding and guitars a-strumming as the caller sang out,

'Oh, I ride with my slicker and I ride all day,
And I pack along a bottle for to pass the time
away. . . .'

Folks had flocked into Duppa Springs from all corners of that northern part of the green and pleasant Tonto Basin, settlers, cowboys, Mex farmers, even a sprinkling of Tonto and Navajo Indians to watch the parades, rodeo and pony races, see the fireworks and listen to the speechi-

15

fyings. In the evening, they had drawn up their wagons in a circle around the dancing platform and barbecue where a steer was being roasted on a spit.

'Ain't that JayCee Lanchester's daughter?' a woman asked, as two young ladies arrived driving a buggy, accompanied by three horsemen. 'What's she doin' slummin'?'

There was a ripple of interest as heads turned to examine Margarita Lanchester in her embroidered white dress of finest cotton, nervous and haughty as a racehorse, her shimmering black hair and classical Spanish beauty tempered by her father's Anglo blood. Lanchester was one of Arizona's richest and most powerful ranchers who ran a big spread at the southern end of the Basin where the grass was greenest.

She was with her cousin, Sarah Navarro, a girl of similar Spanish looks, but plumper and plainer in a wholesome manner, whose mother ran the general store in Duppa Springs. Margarita's own mother had died in childbirth and she had been raised, an only child, by her father. Highly protective of her, JayCee Lanchester had reluctantly allowed her to take this trip north, escorted by his men, to visit her aunt and Sarah.

Margarita might be his only official child, but that was not to say JayCee did not have a score of other progeny scattered about Arizona. He had never remarried, but he had certainly not remained celibate. And one of these, a young and handsome *vaquero*, Tonio Cortez, rode with her escort.

'Come on, girls,' he called, swinging from his mustang. 'You can mingle but don't stray far. And don't let none of these bozos git too familiar. Look at 'em swing those gals like they was bales of hay. Dumb hicks. Me, I'm gonna git us something to eat and drink. We meet back at the wagon. OK?'

'Sure, Tonio,' Margarita smiled. 'You run along. We can take care of ourselves.'

'No, we don' need heem breathing down our necks,' Sarah agreed, as she watched him head towards the drinks table. 'He watch you like a hawk, don' he, Rita? How you stan' that?'

'Aw, Dad's probably instructed him to. Tonio's trying to get in with him. He is my half-brother, after all.'

Suddenly her dark eyes clashed in the glow from the barbecue bonfire with the Pacific blue ones of a tall cowboy, that is to say, a young man who from his rig she took to be a cowboy. He had removed his high-crowned Stetson and his long, flaxen hair fell across his suntanned brow. He raised a hand and swept it back to the knot of the star-spangled bandanna around his neck. He wore a blue, double-fronted shirt and jeans. His high-cheekboned face was intelligent, but with a kind of wistful look as he met her gaze, his eyes stone-steady. Margarita, too, stood on the buggy as if petrified as she stared at him across the other heads.

*'With my feet in the stirrups and my hand on
the horn,
I'm the best darned cowboy that ever was born,'*

The caller crooned, bringing her back to reality.
'Oh, goodness,' Margarita whispered, as she
remained poised to jump down from the buggy, for,
before she could break away from his gaze, the tall
stranger had taken the initiative and was shoul-
dering his way through the crowd towards her.

'Howdy, miss,' he grinned, in an easy-going way.
'It's sure nice to set eyes on you. Care to dance?'

He was holding out a hand to assist her from
the high-wheeled buggy, but a blush rose to
Margarita's cheeks as she hesitated. 'I don't know
you. I mean, we haven't been introduced.'

'The handle's Cal Jones.' His lips smiled in a
sensitive, amused way, and the blue eyes twin-
kled. 'I've a small spread to the north end of the
basin. Up along the Mogollon Rim.'

'Cal?' She tested the name. It seemed as easy-
going as him. She offered her fingers. 'OK.'

He helped her down and, his hand firmly
enclosed over hers, he led her across through the
throng to the low plank platform. Margarita
suddenly had the sensation she would be glad to
go with him anywhere. A dance was just beginning, two lines facing each other, one of men, the
other of girls and women in their rough calico
dresses. 'You go join the opposite end,' Cal
drawled.

The fiddles whined like a cat's chorus in the summer air and they were away, Cal and Margarita the first to go. He went sashaying along the line, arms folded and his boots kicking, and back to his place, and the girl did the same, smiling as the men hooted and yelled. Then they went springing forward together and the tall stranger was scooping her up in his arms and whirling her around. Dizzily, she skipped back to her place to let the second-in-line take their turn, clapping and smiling as she met Cal's eyes.

It was wild, rousting fun. Indeed Margarita could rarely remember having had such fun since childhood, and she was hot and flushed by the time the reel was done. Then, Cal's arm was around her waist and they were jumping down from the platform to go get themselves a couple of glasses of iced punch from the stall. And, as if of one accord, they eased themselves out of the crush back into the darkness and leaned against a wagon-side.

They sipped their drinks, listening to the crescendo of noise around the barbecue, but in a world of their own. Margarita breathed in the cool prairie breeze and gazed up at the sparkling firmament of stars. 'Don't you sometimes think there's another world out there?' she whispered.

'I guess everybody wonders about it sometimes,' he replied, an odd intonation to his speech, possibly Scottish, or Irish, she wasn't sure. 'Up along the Rim, sittin' around the camp-fire nights, we have plenty of time to star-gaze.'

'How long,' she asked, 'have you had your spread?'

'Not long. I'm from Texas. Lost every dang thing I had in the big slump. I ain't complainin'. It ruined bigger men than me. I'm just tryin' to start anew.'

'I guess it must get pretty lonesome out under the sky most of the time,' she prompted.

'No. I don't feel lonesome. I feel at home. Least, I did' – he put his glass on the wagon tailboard and removed hers from her hand – 'until just now, 'til I met you.'

'What are you doing?' she asked, breathless, for he was putting his arms around her and pressing himself up against her, his face serious in the moonlight, watching her intently. 'No, really, I hardly know you. You don't even know my name.'

'Your friend called you Rita. Sounds nice. That's what I'd like to call you, if you'd let me.'

'Wouldn't you like to dance with my friend?' Flustered, the girl wanted to distract him, pressing her hands against his chest to hold him away. 'I'm just visiting.'

'No. Yours is the face I want to gaze at. The prettiest face I ever done seen. I feel like I'd like to spend the rest of my life gazing at you.'

'Really?' she asked. 'You . . . you're not just teasing me?'

'Hell, no, why should I do that?' He stooped his head and tenderly kissed her. 'You're a gosher.'

The caller's words drifted to them:

'Oh, I know a gal who's gonna leave her mother
All the devils below couldn't stir up such a
lover.'

Cal grinned and said, 'That sure is so.'

'I don't have a mother. But I might well leave my father.'

The kiss had landed on her nose because she, a well-brought up young lady, turned her head away. At nineteen, she had never been kissed before by a man. 'I . . . you make me feel strange.'

'You want me to stop?'

For reply, with a mixture of awe, reluctance and willingness, she raised her face tentatively to his, closing her eyes as his lips pressed on hers. And then there was no stopping them. They entwined themselves into each other like they never wanted to be parted.

'Cal,' she murmured, 'for some reason, as soon as I saw you, I felt the same way about you.'

'Like a bolt of lightning hit you?'

'Yes, I suddenly came alive.'

'You seen Margarita?' Tonio asked Sarah, spinning her roughly around to face him. 'Where the hell she got to?'

'That tall *hombre* asked her to dance.'

'Tall *hombre*? Who?'

'Jones, he is called. He come into the store some

time. He run sheep up on the Rim.'

'A sheepherder?' Tonio's handsome face showed his disgust. 'A stinkin', lousy sheepherder asked her to dance?'

'He OK,' Sarah beamed. 'He a nice guy.'

'Nice guy? Are you mad? Where are they now?'

'I theenk I see them go behind that wagon over there,' Sarah simpered. 'Why don' you leave her alone? Why you wanna stop her havin' fun?'

Tonio pushed her aside and strode across past the barbecue. As the big yellow moon came from behind a cloud he saw them in each other's arms alongside the wagon. 'Hey,' he shouted, jerking out his silver-engraved Smith & Wesson. 'You take your filthy hands off that gal.'

'Tonio, what do you want?' the girl exclaimed, as Cal turned from her, spreading the fingers of his left hand when he met the fierce regard of the young man thumbing the revolver.

'I'm taking you back. You jest git away from her, mister. She don't want no truck with no lousy sheepman.'

'Maybe you should let her speak for herself.'

'Sheepman?' Margarita could not stifle the horror in her own voice. All her life her father had expressed his disgust of such people. 'You're a sheepman? Why didn't you tell me?'

'You never asked. What difference does it make?'

'Oh, it makes a difference,' Tonio spat out. 'Step away from him, Sister, before I shoot him down like the filthy dog he is.'

'No! Don't be such a fool. What are you talking about?' The girl stepped towards her half-brother, waving her finger. 'Go away. Leave us alone. What right have you to spy?'

'You're coming with me.' Tonio grabbed hold of her dress and hauled her behind him. There was a ripping noise as the material tore and she was hurled to the ground. 'I'll deal with this galoot.'

'Will you?' Cal Jones had caught the youth's wrist in an iron grip, twisting the gun away, and crashing his right fist into Tonio's jaw, sending him sprawling. As he tried to get to his feet, Jones's boot pinned his wrist to the ground and he kicked the revolver away beneath the wagon. He raised his fist. 'You want another?'

'Don't!' Margarita was trying to cover her exposed breasts with the torn dress. 'Cal, *please*, leave him be. I've got to go. I'm sorry.'

'You fool,' Tonio sneered, as Cal stood back and let him get to his feet. 'Don't you know who she is? JayCee Lanchester's filly. He'll have you churned into mincemeat you touch his gal.'

As Tonio ducked away to search for his expensive revolver, Margarita hesitated, staring at the tall Texan. 'It's the truth. He will, Cal. I'm sorry. Thank you for dancing with me, for everything.'

'Rita,' Cal called. 'Jest 'cause you're Lanchester's gal that ain't the end of everything. We gotta talk this through.'

'It . . . it's not possible.' She blinked tears from her eyes, held her hands over her breasts as she stared at him, then turned and hurried away.

Tonio emerged from beneath the wagon, the gun in his hand. He rubbed at his aching jaw and scowled. 'You, you try to see her again you're dead meat.'

'Aw, go to hell, sonny boy. Don't tell me what to do.'

Three

'Sheep!' A cowboy was screaming the word as he galloped out of the plain into Duppa Springs. He was riding hell for leather, quirting his pony from side to side, his hat-brim bent back by the breeze. 'Sheep!'

It was a word that would send a shiver down any rancher or cowhand's back, and those sitting in the Hashknife Saloon were no exception. They ran out as the cowboy slithered his bronc to a halt to see what was going on. 'Sheep!' the 'poke gibbered, his eyes bulging, hardly able to get the word out. 'That Texan. He's driving 'em down the scarp from the Rim. Driving 'em down from the Mogollons into the Basin.'

'Calm yourself, boy.' Sheriff Alfie Polonski had come running across from his office as fast as his overfed bulk could move. 'Where you seen 'em? What's going on?'

The unwritten law up to then was that sheep-herders, mostly low-down Mexicans, would be tolerated to run their herds up on the scrubby

25

mountainsides that enclosed the Tonto Basin, but woe betide any who tried to bring them down to the plusher grasslands.

'I seen 'em,' the cowboy stuttered. 'I was scouting around up the northern sector when I seen 'em. Thousands of 'em. A white flood of sheep pouring over the Rim and down into the valley. They were being driven by that Texan, Cal Jones, and four of his Tonto herders. They were pushing them down into the valley as fast as they could go. It's his challenge.'

The 'punchers and townsfolk who had gathered to listen stood in stunned silence. It was a long established fact that the whole of the Tonto Basin was the domain of cattle. 'What are we waiting for?' a man shouted. 'Let's go get 'em.'

Tonio Cortez had been drinking whiskey and playing poker in the saloon with two of Lanchester's hands, who had accompanied him. They had been waiting for Margarita to be ready, to escort her back to the JayCee ranch near the township of Riba at the southern end of the Basin. They strolled outside to see what the commotion was about.

'Sheep!' To Tonio it was like uttering a dirty word. 'Them stupid, woolly, bleating, scrubby, useless creatures that destroy the grass, pollute the drinking holes, that all men hate? The Texan must have gone mad-dog crazy. He's asking for war.'

'Hold on.' Sheriff Polanski raised his hands to

quell the shouts of agreement. 'We don't want none of that wild talk. This will have to be settled legally, by due process. I'll ride out tomorrow and see what's going on.'

'Tomorrow's no damn good,' Tonio said. 'You gotta stop 'em 'fore they git to the water.' He gave a whistle of awe as he watched the cowboy unsaddle his lathered-up pony. 'This boy's rode all this way to warn us.' He slapped the stag-horn butt of his revolver. 'This is the only law a Texan understands. The law of the six-gun.'

'I told you to quit that kinda talk,' Polanski roared. 'Simmer down. We ain't gettin' drawn into a shooting match. That sorta thing could flare up, set the whole range ablaze. I might remind you there's more than one sheepman around here. All we got to do is go and warn 'em to get those sheep back.'

Tonio, in his black silk shirt and pants, his silver-enscrolled boots, spat into the dust. 'And what if they don't?'

'Waal,' the sheriff blustered, 'I'll invite 'em to come in for a town meeting. We'll sort this out.'

'A town meeting?' Tonio sneered. 'Are you joking?'

'I ain't telling you again,' the sheriff said. 'You git back to Riba. I don't want you stirring up trouble behind my back. We'll handle this legally. Fer Chris' sakes, this is 1885. We live in the modern world. This ain't what they used to call the Wild West. We're civilized people.'

Margarita had walked across from her aunt's
store, a shawl around her shoulders. 'What's going
on, Tonio?' she asked. 'Are you ready to leave?'

'Not just yet,' Tonio muttered. 'You hang on
here. We got business to attend to.'

Tonio swung a saddle onto his fiery dapple-grey
mustang and jerked his head at his two
compadres. One was a staring-eyed, lank-haired
youngster, Billy Josephs, a bully and braggart,
always ready for mischief. The other was a sullen,
middle-aged 'puncher, Sam Bevans, his face as
leathery as the worn gloves on his fists, a man
whom few cared to cross. He had worked for
JayCee Lanchester for a long time, and could be
depended on for any dubious assignments. He
hung a twelve-gauge shotgun from his saddle
horn, jerked the cinch tight and climbed aboard
wearily. He jerked his sweat-stained hat down
over his brow, and spurred his horse after the
other two. They went at a fast lope out of town,
headed north. Margarita bit her lip anxiously, as
she watched them go. She wanted to chase after
them in the buggy and remonstrate with Tonio,
but she knew it would be no use. They were looking for trouble, and there was dread in the pit of
her stomach at the thought of what might occur.

The three JayCee cowboys rode for the most
part of the morning up into the desolate foothills,
gradually nearing the steep escarpments of the
Mogollon Rim. When they reached a ramshackle

ranch house they were challenged by the ragged nester, Blade Tilbury, and his son, Noah.

'What you want?' he demanded of the men who worked for the rich rancher at the more fortunate end of the valley.

'You heard about the Texan?'

'Sure I heard. But why should that worry *you*?'

'You heard of the thin edge of the wedge?' Tonio asked. 'Thass what this is. Once we let 'em make a start they'll drive in deeper and deeper. That's why this concerns JayCee Lanchester. Who the hell this Texan think he is? He's gotta be stopped. You gonna ride with us?'

Blade Tilbury scratched his grey-stubbled jaw, his weathered face etched by sun and hard times, the result of trying to carve out a living running his small herd of longhorns on this harsh terrain. 'I dunno. I don't want no trouble.'

A scrawny woman, in a faded dress and sun bonnet, had come from the ranch house. 'Blade, don't go with 'em,' she called. 'There'll be shooting. Don't take the boy.'

'Ma,' Noah shouted. 'We gotta defend our land.'

'Yeah, we've gotta protect ourselves,' Tilbury growled. 'I'll go git my rifle.'

The three cowboys ignored the screeching imprecations of the woman as father and son sorted themselves out horses and guns.

'Let's ride,' Tonio said, and they set off into the hills.

*

To some eyes, it might have seemed an idyllic scene. A Tonto herdsman was piping at a flute in his fingers as he sat on a rock and idly watched his strung-out flock of sheep. It was a peaceful out-of-the-way place, a good way from the Tilbury ranch house, albeit much further down the valley than they would normally have grazed. The sheep were spread out along the boulder-strewn domain, their neck bells jingling melodically, occasionally giving a bleat one to the other as they found a tasty thistle.

Tonio, and the four horsemen, appeared on the skyline and hauled their broncs in. 'Goddam, there they are,' he hissed. 'How many's there?'

'About five hundred,' Billy Josephs yelled, 'at a rough guess. I wonder where he's got the rest of 'em?'

'These'll do for a start,' Tonio said, tensing with anger. He had noticed that the far end of the valley terminated in a cliff edge, a sheer 300 foot drop, like many that edged the ravines running from the Mogollon range. 'Come on, boys. Let's drive 'em over.'

They nudged their mounts forward down the steep hillside, giving shrill yips, sending the first of the sheep scattering in front of them. The Tonto, an old but agile man, jumped to his feet and stared at them, leaning on his stick. A headband held his grey hair back from his gnarled face. He had a poncho around his shoulders, a leather bag of belongings on his hip, but, apart from a knife, he was unarmed. His cotton pants were tucked into moccasin leggings. He was accustomed to leaping lightly from rock to rock through cacti and thorns. If he had wanted to he could have probably run off and escaped. But he stood his ground and faced them.

The horsemen were driving whatever sheep they encountered before them, yelling and whipping at them with their lariats, so they had quite a bunch of the alarmed and bleating creatures by the time they reached the Tonto.

'What you do?' he called to them. 'You got no right.'

'It's you who ain't got no right,' Tonio snarled, as he drew in nearby. 'Clear out. Go on. Scram. And tell your boss any sheep found in the Tonto Basin will get the same treatment.'

The Tonto realized they were herding the sheep towards the precipice half a mile away. They already had a good-sized bunch of 300 or so. There were another 200 of them between them and the cliff edge. 'No, you must not,' he cried. He ran to the nearest rider and caught hold of his bridle. 'Go back. This is not right.'

'Take your hands off my hoss, redskin,' Sam Bevans growled. He had the twelve gauge laying across his lap. His eyes, shadowed by his hatbrim, were expressionless, and his bloodless slit of a mouth went with his sullen disposition. 'I'm warning you.'

'No.' The Tonto tried to hang onto the mustang

as Bevans kicked it forward. 'The sheep do not hurt you.'

'Do not hurt us?' Noah Tilbury shouted, his face contorted with anger. 'What you mean? We already found their footprints round our water-hole. We're getting 'em outa here.'

'Git outa my way.' The saddle gun barked flame and the old Indian fell back with a howl of pain, writhing in the dust. Bevans finished him with the second barrel and he lay still. 'He had his chance to get out,' he muttered.

Blade Tilbury stared at the dead Tonto, disturbed. He had not wanted that. But he pulled his old Colt .45 and fired at a sheep, dropping it dead in its tracks. The others panicked and fled. It was amazing how fast sheep could run when they were scared. 'Yee-haugh!' he yelled, and kicked his horse after them, loosing the rest of the shells in his cylinder, excitedly. The other men joined in, chasing after him, pulling their revolvers, too, and creating noisy mayhem, the explosions reverberating through the hills. The herd was going full-tilt, bolting and scrambling over the rocks, heading away along the valley, encouraging those before them to run, too. Now they were a great seething mob chasing blindly one after the other towards the precipice. 'Haugh! Haugh!' Blade shouted, out of bullets now.

When the leading sheep saw their danger and tried to veer away, scramble back, it was too late. The ones driven from behind pushed them on by sheer weight, and they went tumbling and spinning over the precipice, a great yellow-white waterfall of leg-clawing wool, their bodies bouncing off the rocks far below, to lie still in a huge pile.

Tonio pulled in his horse at the cliff edge, breathing hard and grinning as he looked down. There couldn't be many left alive. 'That'll teach him,' he sang out.

There was the crack of a rifle shot from higher up the wall of the Rim, and an answering clap as the sound bounced off the cliff. Almost simultaneously, the slug whistled past Tonio's head, making him duck down and whirl his horse around. He looked up at the cliff, his eyes alarmed, and detected the puff of smoke half a mile up among the scree. There was another clap, another puff of gunsmoke, and a bullet whined through the air, ploughing into his grey's chest, gouging blood. The mustang stumbled and collapsed, throwing Tonio, rolling from the saddle dangerously close to the cliff edge. Inches away from the big drop he managed to claw hold of a rock and haul himself back. 'Shee-it!' he gasped.

More bullets were whistling and whanging, chiselling the rocks about them, as the marksman up above levered the slugs in his rifle magazine. 'He's got the drop on us,' the mad-eyed Billy Josephs screamed. 'Come on, let's git outa here.' He put out an arm to swing Tonio up behind him and they rode off down the slope, hastily followed by the three other sheep-killers. They didn't pause until they were well out of range of the rifleman.

'Yee-ha!' Noah screamed. 'I guess that's taught him a lesson he won't forget.'

'I ain't so sure, son,' old Tilbury muttered. 'That Texan sure knows how to use a gun. He coulda kilt a couple of us if he'd had the mind. I guess we're lucky to be alive.'

'Arr, where's your spunk?' Billy jeered. 'He'll be scared shitless now. He won't try bringing his sheep down again.'

'That was a hundred-dollar hoss he killed,' Tonio cried, indignantly. 'But I guess he's lost a few dollars more than that. With any luck the bozo'll be outa business for good.'

'Come on.' Sam Bevans sat his horse and reloaded both barrels of his twelve gauge. 'We better be gittin' back.'

The lanky Cal Jones climbed down the mountainside, his rifle in his hands. At the cliff edge, he paused by the dead horse and peered down. He thought he heard a bleating sound and detected a slight movement among the huge pile of carcasses at the foot of the ravine. He pursed his lips and shook his head as his partner, Randy, came riding up from along the valley. He had the body of the dead Tonto sprawled over the back of his saddle.

Randy dropped him down, spat, and wheezed. 'Didn't I warn you this would happen?'

Cal stared at the dead Indian, knelt down and closed his eyes. He shook his head again. 'I never thought they would be so damn evil.' He stood tall and peered down over the cliff. 'Come on, let's go down, see if there's any we can save.'

'Cal, I'm quittin'. That's a quarter of our dang stock dead. It ain't no use tryin' to save a few. You've bit off more than you can chew, boy, an' I don't want no part of it. This may be a free range but these cattlemen will run you off it. And if you refuse to go, be sure of one thing: they'll kill you.'

Jones's fierce blue eyes met the old man's and he sighed. 'Fair enough, Randy. But they ain't running me off. I'll send your share to your bank in Tucson.'

As his partner turned his horse, Cal called out, 'You gotta go back through Duppa Springs. Will you do me a favour? Tell the sheriff I want a meeting with him. And, if you see that Margarita Lanchester, tell her I want to speak to her. I'll wait at noon tomorrow outside town at Manzanita Canyon.'

'You're asking for more trouble, Cal.'

'Yeah, I guess.'

Four

Tonio Cortez peered down into the canyon of gnarled manzanita trees and watched the girl he had followed from the town of Duppa Springs. A lock of thick black hair swung across her face and glistened like a raven's wing in the harsh sunshine. She was driving the dainty high-wheeled rig, flicking a light whip across the back of a high-stepping, black, four-year-old. Tonio stepped down through pungent-scented juniper bushes to get a better view. He drew back, sharply, behind a rock when he caught sight of a rider approaching from the direction of the northern rim of the Tonto Basin, out of sheep country. He levered his Winchester carbine and clacked a .44-40 slug from the magazine into the breech, thumbing the hammer and peering along the sights at the Texan.

Tonio's black shirt and pants absorbed the stunning heat of the midday sun and a bead of sweat trickled down his temple from beneath his flat-crowned black Stetson. Maybe it wasn't the heat, maybe it was nervousness. Tonio was a snappy dresser, the yoke of his black shirt and high-heeled boots heavily decorated with silver. In the tooled gunbelt around his waist, was the silver-engraved, $200 Smith & Wesson 'shooter. His high-cut cheekbones retained the bloom of youth and his hair tumbling over his nape was as thick and glossy as the girl's. Indeed, he was almost as good-looking as her. To be sure, he was her half- brother, but there was to Tonio one bitter difference: she was legitimate; he wasn't.

'Cal!' The anxiety and tenderness in the girl's voice rang out through the canyon as the rider approached and Tonio Cortez spat out the gall it brought to his throat. 'Cal! Are you all right?'

As if in spontaneous harmony, the girl, in her blouse and bell-shaped skirt, and the tall horseman, in his sweat-stained shirt and tattered chaps, had leaped to the ground and were in each other's arms as they met, the man sweeping away his stetson and holding the girl firm, putting his lips to hers. To Tonio it looked like their kiss would never end, like they were kissin' crazy. Yeuk! He spat silently again into the weeds. Kissing a sheepman! How could she? Had she no pride? Surely the guy's sheep-stink should repel her. But, no, they were nuzzling and fondling and murmuring low so, as hard as he strained, he couldn't hear what they were saying.

Kill him now, a voice in his mind said to him. Get it over with. It's for her own good. And his trigger finger took first pressure as he aimed at the patch of sweat on the back of the sheepman's shirt, for Cal had swung the girl around, and, all unaware, was shielding her, offering his back as a perfect target. But, no! What if the bullet ploughed through the sheepman into the breast of the girl he was holding, which at that range was more than possible. What if he killed her, too?

Tonio jerked away the Winchester and released the trigger pressure. 'The poor sap,' he muttered. 'We can get him any day.'

What disarmed him as much as anything was the obvious pleasure the girl, Margarita Lanchester, was taking in the man's caresses, glued to him like she could never let him go, peering up into his face. It was obvious she was as head over heels in love with him as the lanky bozo was with her. It rankled in Tonio's guts. 'What the hell she see in him?'

But Tonio was no fool and, as he watched them walk, arms around each other's waist, over to a fallen tree and sit down, conversing tenderly, he knew what she saw in this stupid average Joe: all those dumb qualities he despised – decency, honesty, sincerity, bovine adherence to the work principle, do a hard day for a few honest bucks and sleep sound, always give a feller a helping hand, or, if he ever got into a fight, a fair chance. Christ! He probably raised his hat to the ladies when he went to church on Sundays, was gentle to females and animals, and – for all he knew, horror of horrors! – didn't drink, gamble or cuss.

'What'n hell's matta with her?' Tonio whispered. 'I gotta git back and tell JayCee. She's got it bad. We gotta put a stop to this.'

But, what also rankled with Tonio was that he couldn't either kill the guy, or ride hell for leather back to the ranch. He had to stay and watch this puke-provoking dilly-dallying to the conclusion. Margarita's safety was uppermost. Tonio had been appointed her shadowy bodyguard. He had to watch out for her. But, at the same time, he was watching out for himself. For, if anything happened to Margarita her father's wrath would be the wrath of hellfire. In the past couple of years, Tonio Cortez had ingratiated himself with J.C. Lanchester. It was his plan to be accepted as his true and legitimate heir.

'We sure don't want no damn sheepherding nohoper upsetting the apple cart.' Tonio wiped the sweat from his suntanned brow as he poked his Stetson back with a forefinger and laid the carbine aside. He bared his teeth in a white flashing leer as he watched the couple through the red and green boughs. They had taken to kissing and touching each other again after the earnest talk. But it was all above the belt. Cal Jones was one of those dumb creeps who believed in showing respect in his courtship. 'Jeez!' Tonio snorted. 'I'd have had her on her back by now.'

'*What?*' James Charles Lanchester hissed like a

sidewinder about to strike. 'You say my daughter
was kissin' and canoodlin' with that sheep trash
for two hours all yesterday afternoon and you did
nothing to stop them?'

'What could I do, JayCee? She's got a bad case
of the heart-flutters. They both have. We have to
tread softly here. Two people who think themselves in love don't take kindly to being torn
apart. We have to—'

'Don't tell me what *we* have to.' Lanchester had
somewhat the air of a rattler, grey eyes cold as
obsidian, tense in his movements as if he had a
spring coiled inside him. His features, strong and
straight, were disinclined to smile, unless it were
in a falsely sentimental way whenever his daughter hove in sight. His greying hair was combed
back harshly against his scalp and he wore a
tight, figure-hugging suit of vari-coloured
threads, his linen immaculate. He sat in a private
booth of the Red Rays saloon in the town of Riba.
A waiter was serving him slices of cold salt beef.
'Cut the pickles,' he growled. 'Whadja think I am,
some Mex? How many times I have ta tell ya, I
don't like my food hot.' Carefully he sliced a
portion, putting it into his mouth, nodding
approval, so the waiter poured him a glass of
wine. 'Did I ask you to join me, Tonio?'

Tonio had slid into the booth beside his father,
and had fingered a spare glass forward for a drop
of the wine. He jerked like a startled horse and
backed out of the booth to stand uncomfortably

before the table like a scolded boy. He was aware of some men slumped over the nearby bar watching and sniggering.

Lanchester jabbed his knife at his bastard and snarled, 'It's I who tells you what to do, Tonio. Not you me. Please do not use that term *we* again. It offends me. *We* have to tread softly here. Huh!'

'It's the truth, JayCee. You go storming like a bull out of a chute at a rodeo you gonna do more harm than good. Margarita's a sensitive girl. She could be badly hurt by this.'

'I would ask you not to use my daughter's name so familiarly. She is Miss Lanchester to you.' Primly, the rancher carved some neat pieces and chewed on them, sampling the white Californian wine, nodding assent to the Latino waiter to recharge the glass. 'You, Tonio, are just the son of some Mex whore. You have no parity with my daughter, although you might dream you have. Might I remind you that Margarita is the heiress to a large fortune? She will have no truck with some down-and-out sheepherder. The sooner we nip this infatuation in the bud the better.'

'I'm just saying it ain't gonna be easy. You cain't just blast the guy apart. How do you think Marga—, Miss Lanchester would react, especially if she thought you were behind it? It would be you who was torn apart.'

'All right, Tonio, you may sit down. We don't want the whole town hearing about this.' Lanchester signalled to the waiter. 'Have those drunken fools at the bar thrown out. I don't care for their attitude.'

'Yessir, Meester Lanchester,' the waiter said, and hurried off to speak to the bouncer.

'You may help yourself to the wine if you wish, Tonio. There is no need to try to do so sneakily. And please, remove your hat in my presence.'

'Sure, thanks, JayCee, no offence.' Tonio hurriedly whipped off his low-crowned hat, filled a tumbler and grinned. 'I guess a hat is the last thing a true Westerner takes off and the first he puts on in the morning.'

'A truly trite comment, Tonio. You consider yourself a true Westerner, do you? Well, let me tell you this, the true West has no room for stinking sheepmen. Their very odour poisons our wells.'

'It sure does, JayCee.' Tonio Cortez pushed fingers back through his luxuriant curls and smiled, glad to be accepted in the plush maroon-velvet comfort of the private booth, to be seen to be a crony of his powerful father. The cowhands were being noisily ejected, but none dared throw a punch, or pull a piece in the presence of JayCee Lanchester, although they glowered across at them, venomously.

Lanchester carefully finished his meal and raised his glass to his lips, holding it two-handed as he sipped, thoughtfully. 'Tonio, maybe you're right. Arrange a meeting for me with this scumbag Jones. Perhaps we should use the velvet-glove technique.'

'I'm sure glad you see it that way, JayCee. Softly, softly, killee monkey. Ain't that what they say?'

Margarita sat in her bedroom window brushing her hair as the setting sun flooded the plain with a roseate glow. She had been trained to brush her hair for twenty minutes morning and evening to make it ripple and sparkle with life. It was rather bothersome, but she had little else to do. Her maid, Antonia, was laying out her satin evening dress. Margarita had a vast wardrobe of dresses and changed three times a day. Her morning dress would be of light, embroidered cotton for the house; then she would change into an afternoon dress and large hat to go out riding in the coach. Her father would not allow her to ride horseback. It was unladylike and dangerous: many riders had been killed, or crippled for life. He would have had a fit if he had known that she had been learning to drive Sarah's buggy. He forbade his daughter to enter the kitchens with the result that she barely knew how to boil an egg. She was waited on hand and foot by the large staff in the big old adobe ranch house. She occupied herself with piano-forte and dancing lessons, embroidery and needlework, or reading what books her father deemed suitable. Hers was, she reflected, a cosseted, idle existence. She completed the requisite brushstrokes and sat in her silk pantalettes and lace-trimmed bodice – wondering what

jewellery to wear that night. Did it matter? It
would only be for her father's eyes.

Suddenly, she tensed inside when she spied
him riding towards the ranch house through the
knots of cattle dotting the plain. Straight-backed,
precise, he rode in the manner he performed most
of his actions. He would have lunched at the
saloon he owned in Riba. Margarita had heard a
rumour that it was also some sort of bordello with
five or six unfortunate women available in the
upper rooms. It was hard for her to imagine what
kind of degradation they had to undergo. She was
forbidden to enter the place, but sometimes, as
she passed, she looked up and heard men's
raucous laughter and female screams, presum-
ably of simulated pleasure. She wondered if her
father indulged. She could not imagine him showing any kindness to the girls. He was a strict
authoritarian. Probably he would enjoy whipping
them, she thought, and was shocked that she
could have such thoughts.

She watched her father swerve his fine thor-
oughbred beneath the 'JayCee Ranch' sign over
the gate, come trotting in, jump down and throw
the reins to a groom. Despair filled her at the
prospect of going down to eat dinner alone with
him. After nineteen years of his company she had
begun to feel that she was his prisoner.

James Lanchester was standing with one arm
resting on the big stone fireplace, his other hand
cradling a cut-glass goblet of whiskey, staring into

the grate. He did not turn when he heard the rustle of her dress, with his customary smooth compliments as to her looks, but stayed silent for some time with his back turned to her. Finally, he spoke softly. 'I've been hearing some distressing news about you, Margarita.'

The young woman stood in the turquoise satin dress toying, nervously, with a silver ring on her finger. 'What do you mean?'

'I mean,' he said, turning to her, his face severe, 'news of your disgracefully unbecoming behaviour with some saddle-tramp sheepman at some hoedown.'

'What do you mean disgraceful?'

'I mean, that the dress and bodice you were wearing were torn. Antonia reported that to me. No, don't interrupt. I presume that this man with whom you made a spectacle of yourself at some common dance, plied you with drink and forced his attentions upon you. You had been drinking, hadn't you? That can be the only explanation for your behaviour?'

'I drank about half a glass of punch. Cal kissed me and I kissed him back. I wanted to. For once in my life I was happy. We made no spectacle. We were discreetly in the darkness until Tonio, your spy, burst in on us. It was Tonio tore my dress apart.'

'Cortez? He touched you? I'll have him flogged, I'll—'

'No, it was an accident,' she sighed. 'He mistakenly thought he was protecting me, I suppose. He threatened to shoot Cal, who was unarmed. I remonstrated with him and Tonio pulled me by my dress behind him. In his excitement, he used excessive force, the dress tore and I fell to the ground. You have no need to chastize Tonio for that. Cal gave him a good right to the jaw.'

'Cal, is it? You seem mightily fond of this man. Didn't it occur to you how I would feel? A sheepman, the most evil, hated breed in the territory? And a Texan to boot. How could you, Margarita?'

'How could I? Haven't you heard what else happened? How Tonio and two of your other thugs attacked Cal's herd, killed five hundred head, drove them over a cliff, and murdered an innocent Tonto drover? That's what you should chastize Tonio for. No doubt he imagined you would be pleased.'

'That served the man right. Cal – what's his other name – Jones? That sounds like an alias, he's probably on the lam for some crime – he must have known he should never have risked bringing his filthy herd down into the valley. Feelings run high among cattle folk. Good God! You know that, Daughter, don't you? You're one of us.'

'I'm not one of anyone,' Margarita protested. 'I am myself. Are you saying that you condone what they did?'

'No, of course not.' Lanchester hurriedly tossed back the remains of his whiskey. 'I would not condone murder. I am a man of peace, you know that. But it is this Jones man who has breached the peace. He asked for all he got. And if I ever hear of him touching you again' – he pointed a finger threateningly – 'he'll get worse.'

'You ever touch him,' Margarita hissed, 'I'll leave this house, I'll never speak to you again.'

Her father stared at her for moments, shocked. 'Come, dear, I would not hurt him. I would merely advise him to go about his business some other place.' He advanced towards her and touched her arm. 'We must not argue. You must see the folly of it all. I mean, a sheepman, a drifter, a down-and-out. It's just not possible. Will you promise me that you will forget this man?'

'I'm not sure I can promise that, JayCee' – she was accustomed to using her father's nickname, sometimes she did not feel like his daughter when he hugged her into him like this – 'Cal is only doing what you did when you first started out, trying to raise a herd, make some cash.'

'There, dear' – he squeezed her more tightly, making her hang her head, uncomfortably – 'it's been a shock, but we can get over this. I blame myself. I should never have let you visit your aunt. She is not the upright woman your mother was. Your mother was a saint. I dread to think what she would have made of all this.' He turned and stared up at the huge oil painting of his wife on the wall. 'We have to try to live the way she would have wanted us to; remember that, Margarita.'

'I think she would have wanted me to be happy.'
The girl was relieved that her father had released
her. How often in her childhood her father had
made her feel guilty, as if it was somehow her
fault that her mother had died, that *she* had killed
her, the only woman he had ever loved. 'Mother
might have wanted me to choose my own man.'

'Come now, girl,' Lanchester said, going to bang
the dinner gong. 'Let's be sensible. Your mother
would have wanted you to marry a good man, a
man of substance in the territory, a man who
could keep you in the manner you're accustomed
to live, a man of acumen, one of our own kind, a
man who could take over the reins of our little
empire when I retire. Not some Texan deadbeat.'

'Father, I wish you wouldn't—'

'OK.' He raised his hand. 'We won't speak about
him again. Ah, the soup. Venison soup.' He tucked
his napkin in his waistcoat, taking his place at
the head of the long banqueting table, his daughter on his right, as a maidservant brought in a
tureen. 'Doesn't that smell grand? What are you
going to play for me tonight, dear? A little of that
tinkly Mozart stuff you've been practising?'

'I'll play whatever you like.' She was poised
over the table, her dark eyes glowing like jewels
in the candlelight. 'But one last question: presum-
ably the man who murdered that Indian is going
to be punished?'

'Punished? Ha!' JayCee grinned as wine was
poured for them both. 'He might be charged. But

do you imagine any jury would condemn a man for shootin' an Apache? Why, ten years ago they would have paid two hundred dollars for his scalp. Grow up, dear. No, better still' – he touched her hand – 'stay as you are. It's better you don't know the ways of the world.'

Margarita lowered her eyes in silence. His fingers on her hand were as cold as ice, and it was as if an icicle had pierced her own heart. She knew she would have to obey her father's commands. It was the only way to protect Cal.

Five

The Texan rode his mustang down from the Mogollon Rim through a landscape that was like much of Arizona, a wilderness of mesquite, sage brush, yucca and stones. In spite of what had occurred he could not help being invigorated because for the first time in his life he knew both the happiness and the despair of being in love. It was as if the whole aspect of his life had changed and he sang in a lusty voice some lines of a popular song.

At the other end of the Tonto Basin, JayCee Lanchester, his men, Tonio Cortez, Billy Josephs, and their sullen sidekick, Sam Bevans, were setting out at a hard lope from the JayCee Ranch, riding through well-fed cattle grazing on rich green gramma grass up to their bellies. They were all headed for the same destination, the public meeting that was to be held in the courtroom at Duppa Springs to enquire into recent unfortunate events.

Margarita watched her father and his men set

out. 'Hot damn, I'm going to see if justice gets done.' She ignored her maid Antonia's pleas, and strode round the house to the stables, ordering the groom, Velasquez, to harness a high-wheeled rig, and put a fast horse in the shafts.

'What will your father say?' Antonia protested. 'You don' know how to drive this.'

'I know. I've learned; I'm not totally helpless.' Margarita jumped up into the seat, smoothed her white lace dress and jerked the wide brim of her straw hat down over her forehead. She took the whip in her hand and cracked it over the filly's ears. The startled horse took off faster than Margarita anticipated and she almost fell off the box as the rig went bouncing away. But she recovered herself, hauled on the reins, cornered the house successfully, and went at a fast trot out through the ranch gates. It was another scorching day, just a few fluffy clouds in the blue sky, but there was a pleasant breeze in her face as she drove. She felt elated. At last she was making her own decisions, and, whatever happened at the enquiry, at least she would see Cal again, if for the last time. It was as if she was drawn to him by some unseen force, unable to stay away.

However, as she wheeled along the trail across the prairie, she did have some doubts. Mostly any longhorns in the way would move off the trail as they saw her approach. But the bull-rutting season had begun, and she drew the filly in and paused when she saw two of these fearsome crea-

tures blocking the trail. She listened to their
primordial bellowing and snorting as the huge
beasts pawed the earth, clashed horns, and rolled
around in steaming puddles of their own urine,
the better to impress the ladies, and then began a
short, fierce fight for dominance, charging at each
other until one admitted defeat and ran off.
Margarita watched, curiously, as the victorious
bull tried to mount a female. Nature was very
strange and rather frightening. Maybe she had
better detour? She guided the rig, bumping out
into the grass, in a half-circle around them, gave
a crack of the whip and set off again, not realizing
the danger she had been in. If one of the half-wild
bulls had taken a mind to charge, there would not
have been a lot she could have done.

But it was a long drive to Duppa Springs and
she went on her way at a spanking trot. 'Dad's
going to get a surprise when he sees us,' she called
to the filly, who waggled her ears back, and tossed
her tail, as if she agreed.

There was a seething anger among the crowd,
mostly cattlemen, cowboys and their women, who
had arrived for the public meeting in Duppa
Springs. It reminded Cal Jones as he rode in of
the low angry murmur of a hive of disturbed bees,
ready to set upon any they regarded as their
enemy. He had seen the same seething discontent
in a Texas lynch crowd before they exploded into
violence. He noticed a small group of sheepmen on

the far side of the main drag who had come to give their support and were, perhaps, wishing now they had stayed at home. There was Juan Chavez, and a couple of his herders, and Ike Ticehurst's clan, three sons and a couple of cousins, whose sheep roamed the north-eastern side of the Rim. And, leaning against an adobe wall in the shade, was old Randy Newbolt, polishing his teeth before he popped them back between his gums.

'Howdy,' Cal gritted out, as he swung down beside them and watered his bronc at the trough. 'You still here? Thought you'd be back in Tucson by now.'

'Aw, I couldn't leave ya to fight ya battles by yaself,' Randy wheezed. 'Who knows what kinda trouble ya'll git yaself in.'

Cal grinned at him, grimly, and drawled, 'Quite a crowd. If looks could kill!' The doors of the courthouse were being opened, which distracted the onlookers, who began to push inside. Cal tied his horse to a hitching rail and said, 'Waal, what we waitin' fer?'

When the Texan and his companions walked in, the folks crammed into the rows of hard benches fell silent. A fat lady, fanning herself, hissed, 'That's him. Cain't you smell the stink of sheep on him?'

There was a titter of amusement, but Sheriff Polanski silenced them, shouting, 'All rise for Colonel Henry Dangerfield, presiding.'

The old Confederate soldier took his place on

the podium, tugged at his grey moustache danglers and announced, 'I want to make it clear from the commencement that this is not a trial. We are here to hear evidence about the death of an Indian known as Razor Nose, and the killing of about five hundred head of sheep belonging to these two gentlemen, Mr Jones and Mr Newbolt. Are the other parties involved present?'

'No, they ain't here yet, Your Honour.'

'Yes, we are,' JayCee Lanchester called out, as he strode into the courthouse, followed by his boys in their clattering boots and spurs. 'I'm as keen to get to the bottom of this as y'all are.'

'Right, let's hear your side of it, Jones,' Colonel Dangerfield said. 'First, let's hear about the Indian. Medical evidence is that he was killed from a distance of two or three feet by shotgun blast. The whole of the left-hand side of the head blown away. Complete disruption of the brain.'

'That's so,' Cal said, after being sworn in. 'He was shot down in cold blood by one of those three men when he begged them not to drive my sheep over the cliff. Another of my Tontos was up in the rocks and saw the whole thing. They were both unarmed and no threat to anybody.'

Cal paused, as he saw Margarita, in her long white lace dress, looking rather ruffled and wind-blown, slip into court. Their eyes met, and she smiled and nodded, and took a seat at the back.

'That ain't true. He's lying,' Bevans growled. 'That Injun was trying to stop me passing and was going fer his knife. What was I expected to do? Let him kill me?'

'Are you publicly admitting that you shot Razor Nose?' Dangerfield asked. 'I should advise you—'

'Sure I shot him down,' Bevan shouted. 'It was self-defence. What would you have done?'

There was a roar of approval from the crowd.

'Order,' Dangerfield shouted, banging his gavel. 'Silence. Let us hear the witness. What happened next, Jones?'

'All I can testify to is riding over the ridge and seeing part of my flock being sent tumbling over the precipice by them three fellas there. They were lucky I didn't kill 'em. I was mad enough to. Many another man would have done. We'd worked hard to raise them sheep.'

'You tried to kill me,' Tonio Cortez shouted. 'You killed my best horse and I dang near went over the cliff, too.'

'A pity you damn well didn't,' Randy wheezed out at him.

'No more interruptions,' Dangerfield said, 'or I'll adjourn this hearing 'til you've all cooled down. Now, Mr Jones, how much would you estimate your loss at?'

'Me and my partner have lost at least a thousand dollars in wool and meat,' Cal said. 'We can't afford that sort of loss. I believe we should be compensated.'

'The cheek of the man!' JayCee Lanchester's crisp voice cut in. 'This damn fool Texan drifter comes into an area where it's a known fact sheep are not wanted and provokes a confrontation. He don't deserve a cent. He should pack up and head for pastures new.'

There was a rousing roar of agreement and stamping of feet. 'In fact, I think he's lucky he ain't been lynched,' Lanchester smiled falsely. 'OK, he's had his say. Now let me set you straight.'

He got to his feet and headed for the witness box. He jerked his thumb at Cal. 'OK, boy, out of it.'

'Yes, step down,' the colonel muttered, taking a quick nip from a silver flask. 'It's for my heart, you know.'

'Sure, Colonel, we all know that,' Lanchester beamed, playing the crowd. 'I wouldn't mind a slug of that for my heart, too.'

He picked up the Bible and brandished it. 'I don't need to swear on the Good Book. You all know that I talk straight. But, I will do: I solemnly swear to tell you the truth.'

Suddenly he caught sight of his daughter and his phony amiability dropped. His face became like a hard mask as he stared at her. 'Margarita! What are you doing here?'

'I came to hear what you would say. Isn't that allowed?'

'I mean, how did you get here?'

'I came under my own steam. Does that surprise you? I do have a will of my own.'

Lanchester regained his composure and flashed

a smile. 'Just like her father, huh, a mind of her own? Well, you, too, Daughter, might recognize the truth of what I say.'

Colonel Dangerfield coughed into his 'kerchief and took another nip. 'All right, Mr Lanchester, let's get to the point.'

'Very well, Colonel, you're not a cattleman, so let me explain how it is. These two animals, sheep and cows, have two different grazing habits. They just can't be mixed. Cattle are mildly gregarious. They wander over the country and their method of grazing is to loop bunches of grass into their mouths with their loose, muscular tongues. This means they don't graze the range very short and it gets time to recover.

'Now, let's take a look at sheep. They move in compact bunches, their edged little hooves cutting up the sod and pounding it hard. Their sharp incisors and the split upper lip enables them to bite off the grass to its roots, or below if they desire. They eat every damn thing in sight. What do you think will happen to the lush grassland of our Basin if we allow them in? It will be turned to dust. And their droppings will pollute our waterholes. These are proven facts. This Texan boy has tossed down the gauntlet. It's he who's endangering the peace. Already we've seen the trouble he's caused getting cowboys riled up. I suggest he takes his lousy sheep back up into the mountains where they belong.'

Cal Jones got to his feet to protest. 'You're

twisting the facts, Mr Lanchester. That ain't the truth, that's surmise. Sheep don't pollute water-holes, no more than cows or horses do. If they're properly tended they don't turn the land to dust. That's nonsense. Why, up in Wyoming, many farmers have found it profitable to run both sheep and cows on their land.'

'So,' Lanchester snapped, 'I suggest you take your sheep, Mr Jones, or whatever your name is, and head for Wyoming.'

'And I suggest, Lanchester,' Cal replied, 'you stop trying to push people around. You may be a big man in these parts, you've grabbed all the best land, the the rest of us have got to make a living as best we can.'

'Grabbed all the best land?' Lanchester yelled. 'Might I remind you thirty years ago I was fight-ing Apaches to safeguard this land before you were even thought about. I don't like your inso-lent tone, boy.'

'No, you don't like anybody standing up to you,' Randy muttered.

Lanchester pointed at him. 'You can shut up, too, mister.'

'Gentlemen, please.' Sheriff Polanski struggled to his feet. 'We're trying to come to an amicable solution here.'

'I'm coming to that,' JayCee Lanchester shouted. 'There is only one solution. I'm going to be generous: I'm going to pay Jones and his part-ner the thousand dollars they claim to have lost.

But there's one condition: they take their stinking sheep and move right the hell out of this vicinity. That is the only way to avert war. And I mean that.'

Cal glanced at Margarita, and down at Randy, and shook his head. 'That is not acceptable. We can't go back up. Not until the rains come.'

'All right, Colonel, you might as well close this enquiry.' Lanchester shrugged and threw up his arms in exasperation. 'This stubborn fool's unwilling to accept good money or good advice. So, all I can say is, let him reap what he sows.'

He stomped off down the aisle and snatched hold of his daughter's arm. 'Come on, Margarita, I'm taking you home.'

'Just a minute, Dad.' She tried to throw off his arm. 'I want to talk to Cal. Maybe I can persuade him to see sense.'

Colonel Dangerfield was banging his gavel as the meeting broke up in confusion, and Sheriff Polanski was roaring, 'I'm warning you all. Anyone steps out of line and causes trouble they're gonna feel the full weight of the law. The last thing we want is a range war.'

'All right, boys, wait outside. Margarita and I are going to talk to Jones.'

As the courtroom emptied, Lanchester nodded at Randy. 'You can clear out, too, grandad. This is between us and him.'

'Anything you got to say,' Cal drawled, 'you can say in front of my pard.'

'What's the matter with you, boy? Do you just like crossing me?'

'I'd appreciate it if you didn't call me boy, Mr Lanchester. I'm not your *boy*. In Texas, that's generally how they address servants.'

Margarita crossed over and took his arm. 'Cal, don't get fired up. Dad's trying to be amenable. It's just his manner. He's made you a reasonable offer. Can't you take the sheep and go?'

'The little lady's talking sense, Cal,' Randy said.

Cal shook his head and stroked back his thatch of fair hair, which immediately swung back across his forehead. He fixed Lanchester with his steady, blue eyes. 'I'd like to take your offer, suh, but we need time. Why can't we have until the rains come?'

'That's not the deal. I want you out now. And, another thing, you are not to see my daughter again. You haven't got the kind of calibre I would look for in a son-in-law. You've been giving her the old soft soap, the music and moonlight. She's a susceptible child. You've been twisting her emotions, turning her against her family.'

'I'm not a child, JayCee,' Margarita said.

'You've no experience of men, dear. You don't know what they're like. This drifter's just tomcatting around. Anyone can see that.'

'I understand you did a good deal of tomcatting around yourself, Dad, in the days after mother died.'

'That was the wildness of grief. Any harbour in

a storm. I had to lose myself. Come along, dear, he's not going to listen to reason.'

'I'm not tomcatting, JayCee,' Cal said. 'I don't go in for that kind of behaviour. Never have. I *have* fallen in love with your daughter and I believe she has similar feelings for me. One day I hope to marry her.'

'Whoo-oo! Ain't he a dilly?' Tonio Cortez had remained behind and was standing at the back, his arms folded. He put on a sneering falsetto as he mimicked, 'I'm in love with your daughter and I believe she has similar feelings for me!'

Cal turned to him. 'You keep out of this, Cortez. I've—'

'Any time you wanna try me,' Tonio jeered, lowering his right arm to lightly touch his revolver butt, 'I'm ready for you. What you make of this hayseed, JayCee? He comes riding in here and thinks he can rope and brand your filly.'

'Yes,' Lanchester smiled, tensely, 'that syrup he's giving out I generally pour over my breakfast waffles.'

'Why don't you talk to me, Mr Lanchester, not that jackanapes you keep as your errand boy?'

'Watch it!' Tonio protested.

'All right.' JayCee Lanchester pulled aside the silver-faced lapels of his frock coat and consulted a gold watch in the pocket of his striped-silk waistcoat. 'We're wastin' time slingin' insults here.' He eyed the Texan. 'Love an' marriage, huh? Do you really think you can afford her? Where you thinkin' of takin' my daughter to live? In some hovel someplace in the hills with your sheep? I might remind you, Margarita is used to the best of everything, fine clothes, fine foods, the most expensive luxuries of life. She's one delicate flower. You think you can make her happy? Forget it, buster. Come on, dear' – he took her arm – 'it's time we were leaving. We have a long ride back.'

'Why don't you let her speak for herself? Every time you use that word "dear" it's like you're putting a knife to her throat. Can't you see she's terrified of you?'

'Listen to him,' Tonio crowed. 'He's as serious as a preacher.'

Cal ignored him and offered his hand to the girl, who was about to obey her father. 'What do *you* say, Rita? When I've got myself better set up, would you marry me?'

Margarita smiled and took his hand, swinging herself into the cowboy's side, staring back defiantly at her father. 'Of course I would. He's the man I want, Dad, I know it.'

'Hell take me!' Lanchester flung up his hands. 'Am I hearing right? Well, well, well . . . we're gonna have to think this over. I never dreamed my l'il gal—'

'I can't be your *l'il gal* forever, JayCee.'

'No, I know. But I was hoping for a man of, say, more distinction. Still, OK, I'll keep an open mind on this. As for you, Jones, you ain't made a very good impression on me so far. But, let's give this time. We all know the old maxim, marry in haste repent at leisure. So, we'll leave it like that, shall we? Come along, dear. All this arguing has made my head ache. Say goodbye. It ain't the end of the world.'

Margarita flashed a smile at Cal, standing on tiptoes to kiss his cheek. 'Whatever happens, I'll wait for you.'

'And me for you,' he said. 'Maybe we're on different sides of the fence right this moment, but it'll work out, you'll see.'

'You bet it will,' Randy hooted. 'The gal's crazy 'bout cha.'

The crowd of burly cattlemen outside had become even more hostile. They parted respectfully to allow JayCee Lanchester through to usher his daughter to her buggy, handing her up. But they glowered, fiercely, at Cal and Randy, blocking their path. Cal's steady blue gaze met theirs and he shouldered his way past, ignoring their muttered challenges, 'Why don't you clear out, like he says?' – 'You're dead mutton, mister' – 'Sheepmen scum, don't you know you ain't wanted here?'

'I thought it was a free country,' Cal said, and pushed through them, strolling across the wide dusty street to join Ramirez and the Ticehurst clan. 'Waal,' he muttered, 'that didn't prove much. We'll see you boys around.'

Tonio Cortez and Billy Josephs were stirring up

the bunch of cattlemen, standing on the sidewalk outside the courthouse, calling out crude insults. Beside them stood surly Sam Bevans, his hard face shadowed by his hat brim, his thumbs stuck in his gunbelt. Suddenly he clutched at his chest and staggered back against the adobe wall as blood began to seep from the arrow in his gloved fist.

A woman screamed, and in the silence there was the hiss of another arrow – *Tzit!* – the feathered shaft thudding into Bevans' two inches lower, penetrating his heart. This time he slid down the wall, his boot heels kicking out, his face agonized. 'It's Tonto vengeance,' a man said, in a hushed voice.

Tonio had his Smith & Wesson double action out, and was poised on his toes, his eyes searching for the assailant. Suddenly he saw him on a rooftop above the sheepmen, a young Indian, the son of Razor Nose, and he was fitting a third arrow to his bow. Tonio fired without hesitation and the Tonto teetered on the roof edge, somersaulted forward, and thudded into the dust, lying prone.

As if a fuse had been applied to a powder keg the gang of cattlemen seemed to explode, hauling out their sixguns and blazing away at the sheepmen on the far side of the road. Women screamed and scurried with their children for cover. JayCee Lanchester leaped onto the rig beside his daughter, snatched the reins and raced the filly away around the side of the livery. 'You wait here,' he shouted. 'Don't move.' He jumped down and ran back to see what was going on.

All hell had been let loose as the sheepmen grabbed their carbines and sixguns and returned fire, backing away to seek cover behind water troughs, barrels and wagons, but they were severely outnumbered and in danger of being mowed down.

'We gotta get out,' Cal yelled, grabbing his horse and vaulting into the saddle. 'Come on. They'll cut us to pieces.' He had no sidearm himself, and was reluctant to bring the heavy .44-.100 Creedmore into action. The only way to defuse the situation was to run.

The sheepmen could see the sense of his argument, as the bullets in their sixguns were quickly dispensed, and ran to hurl themselves on their horses. But young Jesse Ticehurst was not quick enough. A bullet in his back from Billy Josephs bowled him over. He lay there in the dust choking his last on his own blood as the sheepmen raced out of town, kicking up a cloud of dust, a volley of lead whistling about their ears.

'Well, I'll be damned.' JayCee Lanchester gave a whistle of awe. 'They've started something now.'

An eerie silence had descended on the scene as the acrid gunsmoke drifted and those who had taken part in the short, sharp battle stared at the three corpses. And then the cattlemen all began talking and yelling at once as the burly Sheriff

Polanski tried to pacify them.

'Ain't you getting a posse together to go after 'em?' JayCee demanded.

'No, I ain't. Thass only gonna fan the flames. Things are gettin' badly outa hand here, Mistuh Lanchester. Ain't four dead enough? I'm seriously thinkin' it's time I called the army in. We got a war on our hands.'

'The army? Ha!' Lanchester strode across the road to Tonio and Billy Josephs who were standing over the dead Tonto, calmly reloading their revolvers from their gunbelts. 'Yeah,' he said, 'in the old days we'd have taken that bastard's scalp.'

'Poor old Sam Bevans,' Josephs said. 'You and he went back apace, didn't you JayCee?'

'We sure did, Billy. OK, Tonio, you better do the sheriff's job. You'll have plenty of volunteers. Get well armed and get after them. I want that Texan taken apart.'

'You mean like dead?' Tonio asked.

Lanchester nodded. 'Whatever you have to do.'

Margarita ran up to him as the two gunslingers turned on their heels. 'Where are they going?'

'I dunno. You and me, we're going home.' He took her arm and firmly walked her back down the street. 'You see now the trouble that Texan causes.'

Six

They rode at full tilt out of Duppa Springs, quirting their mustangs, hooves pounding the sun-hard ground, racing straight as an arrow across the scorched plain until they reached the northern sector of the Basin and the trail began to ascend through rocky scrub and harsh ravines and they pulled in.

'They got Jesse, Pa,' one of the Ticehurst boys screamed, tears trickling through the dust and grime on his face. 'Ain't we goin' back fer his body?'

'That would be a fool thang to do, and you know it, boy.' Old Man Ticehurst raised his battered hat and wiped the sweat from the bald dome of his head. 'Mood they're in, they'd shoot you down like a dawg. No questions asked.'

Cal leaned on his saddle horn and looked across at the eastern side of the Rim. 'If I were you, Juan, I'd git back to your flock and move 'em up into the mountains, disappear for a bit 'til this blows over.

You been here for generations. They ain't likely to go after you.'

He had spotted a swirl of dust hanging over the trail below. Riders were following, pressing hard. 'It looks like they got a posse together and mean business. We'll head on, draw 'em away.'

'*Adios*,' Juan called, as he and his herders trotted away. '*Vaya con Dios*.'

'Yeah, it looks like we all might be needing His help,' Cal muttered, and set his horse pounding away up towards Snake Pass.

It was about two in the afternoon and hardly a breath of air stirring, the sun high in the sky. The scrubby mustangs of the Ticehursts were foaming at the bit, lathered up, and slowing fast as they struggled up towards a natural spring and waterhole at the entry to Snake Pass.

'They're gaining on us,' Randy Newbolt looked back as he let his horse drink. 'What we gonna do, Cal?'

'I guess it's time we made a stand – this far and no further.' Cal's eyes glinted fiercely, as he looked up at a 200 foot column of rock that jutted out from the ragged cliff of the Rim. 'If we could git our horses up there we could hold 'em off.'

'I'm with you,' Ticehurst said, kneeling at the spring to fill his wooden canteen. 'We cover 'em from up there there's no way they'll git through the ravine.'

'We hope!' Randy glanced at Cal. 'I thought you

said the last thing you wanted was a shooting war.'

'It ain't my choice. It's thrust upon us. What else can we do?'

'Quit yappin' and let's do it,' Ticehurst put in, setting off to climb the ascent on foot, leading his horse. 'I know this place. There's a natural hollow at the top. I kept a few sheep there once.'

His boys trailed after him, dragging their reluctant broncs, followed by Cal and Randy, glancing back to see how close the posse was getting.

The crown of the column of red rock was, indeed, an ideal spot for a bushwhacker. They hurriedly pulled their horses into the cliff's overhang and took up positions peering down at the winding trail below. The riders from Duppa Springs were fast approaching. 'I figure there's about twenty of 'em,' Randy called.

'Yeah, an' there'll be a lot less soon,' Old Man Ticehurst growled, peering down the barrel of his Winchester. 'I'm a man of the feud. Boys, remember Jesse. We got blood to avenge.'

'Hell,' Cal sighed, as he adjusted the sights of his Creedmore and concentrated on the leading horseman, a man in black shirt, pants and hat, silver flashing on his boots. 'This ain't what I wanted, but it seems like they're asking for it.' He had the sights lined up on the heart of Tonio Cortez. He clacked a slug into the chamber and thumbed the hammer.

A bead of sweat trickled down his temple as the

pursuing horsemen trotted up to the spring. He squeezed the trigger, but at the last second averted aim. His shot cracked out, the slug chiselling the rocks by the hooves of Tonio's mustang, making it dance. He *was* Margarita's half-brother, after all. He watched Tonio almost thrown from the saddle, slithering to the ground, grabbing his rifle and running for cover behind a rock.

The Ticehurst clan had no such reservations. They aimed to kill or maim, their shots rattled down, the reverberations bouncing from the walls of the cliff. But they were not particularly skilled marksmen. Their first volley, before they had to reload, injured two of the cattlemen, one in the shoulder, one in the leg. They were dragged away into the shade by the spring, while others hopped around like jack-rabbits seeking cover from the flying lead.

'Yay-hoo!' one of the Ticehurst cousins yelled. 'That sure showed 'em. This is easier'n pottin' coyotes.'

Cal raised his eyes to the heavens and met Randy's gaze. 'Gawd!' he said. 'How did I manage to git us mixed up in this?'

'Tontos believe in an eye fer an eye an' I guess that's what this war is gonna become. You kill one, somebody on t'other sides' gonna kill two back, 'til you start to lose count.'

'Yep.' Cal turned back to the battle and began to do some serious shooting with the long range Creedmore, but somehow his heart wasn't in it.

'Looks like that's the way it is.'

All afternoon the hills echoed with gunshots as rifles and carbines barked out and the pursuers below tried to climb up towards the men 200 feet above, but each assault was driven back, without so far any loss of life.

Meanwhile, the men besieged up on the bare butte were beginning to suffer badly from thirst as the long hot afternoon drew on. The fierce sun moved across the clear sky and blazed down on them. They had fed the last water in their canteens to their mustangs to keep them ready to make a run, for, with hundreds of rounds spent, the defenders were low on ammunition, too.

'We can't hold on here for ever,' Old Man Ticehurst called. 'Sooner or later we're gonna have to make a break.'

Down below, the frustrated posse, which had made several unsuccessful attempts to storm the rocky rampart, at least had a supply of water and, as the great red ball of sun began to drop behind the Rim of the Mogollons, the benefit of some shadow.

Tonio cursed as he looked up at the rocky column and a stray bullet whined past his head. 'There ain't no goddamn way they gonna let us git up there.'

Billy Josephs touched his arm, his lank hair hanging over his crazy eyes, and grinned, pointing to a ridge that ran behind and above the column of rock. 'Maybe if I got up there I could get a bead on 'em.'

Tonio rubbed his swarthy jaw. 'You figure there's a way up? You go for it, boy. We'll cover you.'

As he watched the long-legged cowboy go leaping away, his rifle in his hands, racing towards the far side of the ridge, he muttered, 'He's crazy as a 'coon. No way you'd git me up there.' Tonio was beginning to wish he was back in the comfort of the saloon in Riba and had never had to come on this damn fool expedition after a few lousy sheepmen.

Suddenly the sun bled back across the ridge and was gone and they were engulfed in the strange afterglow. Just as suddenly, a big silver globe of moon began to slide upwards into the night sky. Up on the mesa, Cal ducked back from the shooting to go take a leak and attend to Mosquito. His wool shirt was soaked in sweat and he shivered as a cool breeze swept down from the mountain top. It soon got chill at night in these desert parts. He pulled on his sheepskin jacket, and stretched his limbs, and wondered what would be the best thing to do. Let Lanchester and the cowmen win the day and pull out? Or fight on for his rights to herd his sheep?

He looked across at the ridge of rock about 200 yards away which rose up above them and thought he saw movement. Was that the dark silhouette of a bush stirring in the breeze? Or was it a man crouched on the cliff-edge? Yes, the moon's light shimmered on the blued steel of a rifle barrel. 'Look out,' he yelled. 'Above you to the left!'

Orange flame flashed and one of the Ticehurst boys screamed as lead ploughed into his back. He jumped like a scalded cat and lay still. Cal grabbed up his Creedmore and hugged it into his shoulder, a huge anger seething through him at this waste of life. He aimed at where the flash had come from, at the shadowy shape on the hillside, who was trying to climb away. 'Got him!' he hissed, as he watched the rifleman lose his footing, drop his weapon, almost in slow motion, and topple backwards, bouncing and tumbling, and crashing 300 feet down into scree at the foot of the ravine. He lay still. 'Well, if I didn't get him, he sure dang broke his neck.'

Old Man Ticehurst was kneeling over the body of his dead son. 'That's two gone,' he wailed. 'How'm I gonna tell their ma?'

Cal gripped his shoulder, then strode to the edge, looking down. 'I'd advise you men to pick up your injured, and that dead varmint, whoever he is,' he shouted, 'and head on home. You've killed another of us, ain't that enough?'

'Not until you're dead, too, Texan,' Tonio shouted up, cupping his hands. 'That's two of *my* pals you've killed. We'll be back, doncha worry . . . when you ain't expecting us. You're as good as dead. And don't think you'll ever git your hands on that gal. It's over for you.'

*

The next morning, Margarita was sitting at her window brushing her hair, when she saw Tonio Cortez riding towards the ranch. He had the lead rein of a mustang attached to his saddle and across the mustang a man was slung, hanging lifeless. Tonio cantered into the ranch and hauled the broncs in, stepping down lightly. 'Oh, my God!' Margarita gasped. The lank fair hair hanging down, the long body, the chaps . . . could it be Cal? She ran downstairs and out onto the porch as her father was hauling the head up by the hair to take a look. 'Who is it?' she asked.

'Josephs.' JayCee looked up, sharply. 'Get inside.'

'How about Cal . . . Cal Jones . . . is he. . . ?'

'It was that murderer killed my pal,' Tonio spat out. 'It's time we put out a warrant on your friend Jones.'

'Shut up, Tonio,' JayCee snapped. 'Git him planted in the chapel yard.'

'You gonna speak some words over him, JayCee?'

'No, I ain't. I got better things to do, like breakfast.' The rancher took his daughter's arm and ushered her back into the shadowy house. 'Well, it looks like your young rooster's showing his true killer colours.'

'That's not fair, Dad. If Cal did kill him, it must have been in self-defence. He must have been attacked.'

'Yes, a posse went after them. But it seems they

escaped. These sheepmen are slipperier than snakes. Sit down, dear, calm yourself.' He led her to the banqueting table, seated her. 'Here's a nice jug of coffee and cream. What you having, waffles?'

'No. Just coffee.'

'Margarita, you've got to eat. I've been thinking, it's time you and I took a vacation, got away from here for a while. We could go to California, take a steamer up the coast to San Francisco. They say it's an amazing city. There's all kinda things to see. And lots of society folk. You could go to balls and what they call *soirées*, meet real men, men with money, influence, ideas. It's a man like that you need to wed, not some broken down cowpoke turned sheepherder.'

'Dad,' she groaned, 'I don't want to go to California.'

'Well, if it ain't the men you're interested in, there's some wonderful sights. They say that in that Yosemite Valley there's some waterfall nearly two thousand feet high, great redwoods that blot out the sky. You need to travel, see things, broaden your mind.'

'My mind's been broadened enough the last few days. I've seen how low men can get.'

'You ain't seen nuthin' yet, honey. That's why I say we should get away from this claustrophobic valley for a bit. What's the use of all our cash if we never enjoy it? No, my mind's made up, gal. You better start packing your trunk. Don't bother bringing extra dresses. When we get to California you're going to have the best money can buy.'

'Dad, I don't want to go.'

'Sure you do, honey.' He stood up and gave her a squeeze. 'It'll be good for ya. Sweep all them cobwebs outa your mind. You'll see. You'll thank me. You'll be a different girl. Ah, here comes the post. I been expecting a letter.'

The mail hack, a little sturdy cart and pony, came trotting in, and the local postman tossed a packet to JayCee as he went out onto the porch. 'Thanks,' he called, and tore it open. When first hearing news of his daughter's entanglement with Cal Jones he had enquired where he hailed from and had been told Fort Worth. So he had quickly sent a telegraph to the US marshal of that city asking for information about him. JayCee was not a man to hang about. He had an idea there was something fishy about the Texan, one of the Smith and Jones tribe. 'Ah,' he cried, triumphantly, as he saw the package contained three 'Wanted' notices, expecting to see Cal's features plastered over one. But, instead, they were likenesses of three desperadoes known as the Houck gang. Homicide, rape, bigamy, larceny, forgery, cattle and horse theft, stage robbery, assault with a deadly weapon ... it seemed the list of their crimes was interminable.

JayCee felt vaguely disappointed that Jones was not listed as a member, and turned to a hand-written letter from the marshal for explanation, returning to the breakfast-table and sinking back into his big horn and hide chair.

Dear Mr Lanchester
The tone of your wire come as a mighty big surprise to me. You ask for any information on Cal Jones, his criminal past. Well, as far as I know, he don't have one. In fact, he is regarded highly in this territory. Although only a young man he served with great distinction for six years as a Texas Ranger, rising to the rank of captain. He was several times commended for his personal bravery in tracking down, arresting or killing felons at considerable risk to his own life. One of the vilest of these gangs was that led by Jake Houck (his, and two of his sidekicks' details enclosed). They terrorized honest folk along the Brazos River and beyond until Captain Cal Jones brought them in. Although all three were confessed multiple murderers, by the aid of shrewd Jack lawyers, they managed to cheat the noose and received life sentences. When Rangers have put their lives on the line such results tend to dispirit them. Unfortunately, sir, during that arrest, which occurred in darkness at the gang's hideout, Captain Jones accidentally shot and mortally wounded a comrade officer who got in the line of fire. Jones was acquitted of any blame at a subsequent hearing. However, the incident

played on his mind, I suspect, and he resigned his commission. On leaving, he was presented with a certificate of merit for his services to the state. He went into ranching on a small scale, but chose the wrong year and went bust. I understand he wished to make a fresh start by moving to Arizona. It is a surprise to me that you should suspect he is a man of low principles. On the contrary, here at Fort Worth he is regarded as a man of honour, a man who always gave a criminal a chance to surrender, rather than simply gun him down. That, for Texas, I can tell you, is a rare breed.

> *Yours sincerely*
> *Marshal Jack Cleeve*

JayCee took a sup of his coffee and growled, 'Sounds like the sun shines out of his friggin' ass.'

'What?' Margarita asked. 'Who's that?'

'Nuthin'. Nobody you know.' He returned to the letter's postscript deciphering the longhand scrawl with difficulty:

I have bad news. Houck and his two accomplices broke out of San Fernando long-term prison last month. All have sworn vengeance on the man who arrested them. We have had reports of them committing crimes in El Paso and in New Mexico. It would seem they are heading towards Arizona. I would advise you

*to inform all law enforcement officers in your
area. And I would take it as a favour, Mr
Lanchester, if you would warn Cal Jones of
these facts.*

JayCee gave a whistle of disgust. 'Trouble just
follows that man.'

'Who?' There was concern in Margarita's voice.
She did not normally enquire into her father's
business but she had a strange feeling this might
involve her. 'Who's that from, JayCee?'

'Nothing for you to concern your pretty head
about. But if you really want to know.' He tossed
the three 'Wanted' posters her way. 'It seems three
Texan killers are on the loose and it's figured they
might be coming through the hills into Arizona.
Just a routine warning. They could be anywhere.
But, perhaps that's all the more reason why it's
time you and I took a vacation.'

A maid came in with his waffles, syrup, steak
and eggs, and he folded the letter and posters and
stuffed them in his suit pocket. 'Until then,' he
said, jabbing a knife in his daughter's direction,
'it's best you don't leave the house. No more
taking crazy lone rides on that rig. It's your safety
I'm thinking of, dear.'

Cal was cleaning his rifle, sitting out on the cliff
edge of the Mogollon Rim, not far from their lean-
to. At that altitude a constant wind riffled his fair
hair and bandanna, rattled his chaps. He saw

Randy guiding his bronc through the rocks towards him and called, 'How's the herd?'

'We got 'em all back up and outa danger, but they're in no fit state to drive to market. What we gonna do, pard?'

'That depends. I'm beginning to come to the conclusion that I was wrong and stubborn-headed, and you and Lanchester were right. It was asking for trouble taking 'em down there. A couple of innocent young fellas are dead afore their time. And a couple of not so innocent older ones.'

'Waal, at least you're startin' to see sense,' Randy hooted, hopping down to sit on a rock beside him, and filling his pipe. 'Maybe ya should fergit this durn country, head fer Wyomin'.'

'Maybe I should. But we gotta find a buyer for the herd first. Even then, once we've paid the Tontos their back wages, an' something for the families of them two who died, we ain't gonna have much of a stake to invest. Once a man's gone bust, it sure is a hell of a job to start over again. Others have done it, I know.'

'You shoulda taken that thousand Lanchester offered ya. You've done what he wanted done now, anyhow, brought the critters back up.'

'Aw, I didn't want to take that man's money. He got me mad with his attitude. Who's he think he is?'

'Thass all very well,' Randy piped up through his tobacco smoke, 'but I wouldn't have minded my share.'

'Yeah, OK, I'm sorry. I'll see you right. Strange how a man can be so unlike his daughter.'

'I ain't so sure about that. That gal's got plenty of sass in her, too. Why doncha face it, Cal, she ain't your sort? Why, I doubt she's ever done a hand's turn in her life.'

'It ain't that. It's a thing of minds between us two. But I'm getting your point. To tell the truth I've been thinking it might be best if I went away for a year or two, try to make some honest cash up Wyoming way, see how she feels then. You fancy comin' along, old-timer?'

'Sure, why not? My wanderin' days ain't through yet.'

'You might think I'm giving in easy. But I just want to avoid any more bloodshed. What's the point of it, just over a few sheep and cows?'

'That why you're cleaning that rifle?'

Cal pulled a rag through the barrel and squinted down it. 'Not a speck to be seen. Clean as a whistle.'

'What's that other one?' Randy suddenly noticed a long-barrelled revolver on a rock beside the Texan. 'I ain't seen that before. I thought you didn't carry a sidearm.'

'I swore I never would again. But a man's gotta protect himself, ain't he? I had it hid away back of the lean-to. It's old, but it's solid. Belonged to my father before me, pre-War.' He picked up the heavy Texas Paterson by its worn hickory grip and raised it against his cheek, clicking the cylinder around, listening to the action. 'Smooth as a clock. Good as new. Converted by the Thuer system to brass centre-fire cartridges. I got six trusty friends in here.'

'For a man who believes in peace you're sure gittin' tooled up.'

Cal grinned, and wrapped the Paterson back in its velvet cloth. 'I'll shove it back in the lean-to. I won't be needing it today. I'll take General Crook and move half the herd south along the Rim. You move your half north. Who knows, we might even find some water' – he glanced up at the clear sky – 'but I kinda doubt it.'

Seven

'I'm going out on the range with Pedro,' JayCee snapped at Tonio as he came out of the ranch house. 'You go into Riba keep an eye on the saloon. And keep your thievin' hands off my best bourbon. Tequila's good enough for you.'

JayCee was in his neat town suit. The only concessions he made to the desert were hat, boots, spurs, and bandanna against the dust. He strolled around to the stables where Velasquez had his big grey quarter horse ready saddled. JayCee showed Tonio the mugshots and rap sheets on the Houck gang. 'I've an idea these three varmints might be paying us all a visit.'

'What for?' Tonio raised an eyebrow, somewhat alarmed, as he studied the razor-sharp, narrow-eyed features of Jake Houck, his long list of convictions. 'Who is this crafty-looking bastard?'

'One of the Lone Star State's worst. He'll be looking for Jones.'

'So, what do I tell him, JayCee?'

'You just point him in the right direction.'

Lanchester smiled thinly as he took his horse's reins and swung into the saddle. 'We're gonna let Houck and his cronies do our job for us. They're the answer to a maiden's prayer!'

'There shouldn't be any difficulty recognizing him,' Tonio said. 'It says he has the top of his head shaved and has some kinda pigtail.'

'His first lieutenant, Jurgen Schwarz, sounds pretty distinctive, too. A big fat Hun. Blond curls, boxer's chin, sadistic tendencies. The second lieutenant's a half-breed Texan boy, Jimmy Ramirez. Two fingers missing on his left hand. You can't miss 'em.' Lanchester stuck out his hand for the posters. 'If they should show up give 'em the hospitality of the saloon. I don't want anybody interfering with their plans.'

'This sounds like you're playing with fire, JayCee.'

'What you scared of? We can pick 'em up after they've done what they came to do.' Lanchester rode the quarter horse back and forth in the stable and called out to the groom, 'Velasquez, Senorita Margarita is not to go out driving. OK? You let her go off on her own like the other day, you're out.'

'*Si, señor.*'

'I might be taking a vacation, Tonio.'

'Would that be wise, right now, JayCee, with these bozos about? They might come after our stock.'

'*My* stock, you mean? Yeah, I know, and the

round-up in the offing. But I could leave you in charge, couldn't I? You could handle things in town, and Pedro and the boys out on the range?'

'Sure, JayCee.' Tonio flashed his white teeth, proud to be accepted at last for his worth. 'We can handle things.'

'It's Margarita I'm thinking about. I want to get her away from all this for a while.' A flicker of anxiety crossed JayCee's face as he stroked his fresh-shaven jaw. 'I dunno. I'm in a bit of a quandary.'

'Duh?' Tonio looked blank. 'What's that you're in?'

'I mean it's a problem. Maybe I should go? Maybe I should stay?'

'Yeah, you go,' Tonio grinned. 'These boys, they won't give me any trouble. I can take care of things.'

'Yeah?' JayCee looked doubtful as he held back the sturdy horse's powerful head, then eased the reins and let her go out of the stable at a high-stepping trot. He didn't bother saying goodbye. He didn't want his bastard son to get any fancy ideas that he was going soft on him. Tonio was one of those youngsters who, given an inch, would take a mile. He was too cocky for his own good.

They rode out of the mountains and hauled in their broncos on the lower edge of the Mogollon Rim, six horsemen, peering through the heat-haze across the green fertile Tonto Basin. Their leader,

Jake Houck, put a slim brass telescope to his eye
and studied a cluster of ruddy adobes, those of the
original Latino inhabitants, which stretched out
into a main street of false-fronts and clapboard
cottages. At one end was a white-painted wooden
church with a bell-tower steeple.

'Ain't that sweet?' he drawled. 'A little outpost
of America in the wilderness. So this is where he's
hidin' hisself. What they call this place?'

'Riba.' They had enlisted a Mexican horse-thief,
Raoul Garcia, in Silver City, New Mexico, to guide
them through the high mountain passes and he
pointed to an adobe building like a high-walled
fort five miles distant. 'You see that place? That
ees Lanchester *rancho*. Fine grass, good fat cattle.
That geev you idea, *amigo*?'

'Ai-yee!' Another unsavoury Mexican, Jorge by
name, rustler by profession, who had also joined
them, yelped with glee. 'We take them easy, *si*?'

'Hang on. That can wait. We got personal business first.' Houck removed his wide-brimmed
black hat, with its band of woven human hair, and
wiped the sweat from his shaved head. A single
plaited pigtail hung down to his nape and the
lobes of his satanically pointed ears were pierced
by thick silver rings. He had a double bandoleer of
ammunition criss-crossing his powerful shoulders, and twin Remington revolvers, butts
forward on each hip. He was a man who believed
in the crosshand draw. 'So, boys, we play it cool.
We don't want no trouble with nobody else 'til

we've done what we come to do.'

The big-gutted, Germanic-looking individual, Schwarz, nodded grimly, as did the 'breed, Jimmy Ramirez, their eyes glinting with the anticipated pleasure of vengeance.

'He's gonna have a big surprise seein' us,' Ramirez hissed.

'Ain't we gonna have us some fun down in that town first?' a runty sixth member of the gang, Abel Funt, whined. He wore a battered top hat and an over-long, split-tailed macinaw. An all-purpose no-good, he had joined them back in El Paso.

'Sure we are,' Houck grunted, replacing his hat. 'But don't go shootin' up the town. I don't want nobody ending up in jail. Come on. Let's go. Yah!' He gave a howl and ploughed his mustang down through the shale and heavy timber that clothed the slopes of the Rim at this point and, when they reached the lower ground, headed at a deter-mined lope towards Riba.

'Holy Mother!' Tonio peered from a window on the top floor of the Red Rays saloon and saw six horsemen trotting along the main street. 'It's them. They sure didn't waste no time.'

'Who?' A curvy blonde girl, called LuluBelle, squeezed in beside him, peered through the soft green leaves of the branches of the cottonwoods that lined the street, and squealed as the men passed below. 'Hi,' she called, fluttering her fingers, leaning out in her frothy lace negligée,

'Come up an' see me, boys.'

Houck glanced up and scowled, but little Abel
Funt, at the rear, raised his battered hat and
yelled, 'Yee-how!'

The men rode on, sizing up the town, the bank,
the billiards hall, gunshop, general store and
outfitters, the church and meeting hall, barber's
shop, a few idlers lounging outside watching them
pass; wheeling around the bandstand on the town
plaza they started back and turned into the black-
smith's livery.

'Looks like they're gonna give their broncs a
rubdown and feed,' Tonio said. 'Ugly-lookin'
bunch, ain't they? Still, never mind, gals, they all
can't be handsome like me. Anythan they want,
you give 'em. Y'all ready? Lulu, ain't you had a
bath today? You stink like a polecat under that
perfoom. Not that that will bother 'em.'

The five saloon hussies, Rosemary, a volup-
tuous redhead, Melanie, a scrawny Kentucky
belle, Josepha, a Mexican, her black hair drawn
back severely, a flower behind one ear, Marietta,
her seventeen-year-old daughter, and LuluBelle
were all lounging about the high-ceilinged room
in various states of undress. With the exception of
Marietta they looked somewhat worn around the
edges, magnolia flowers about to fall, bored and
listless with it.

'Come on, gals, brighten up.' Tonio rapped on a
roulette wheel and winked at the croupier. 'Git
ready to roll, Charley.'

He went down the wide staircase of the big old adobe house. At this time of the morning there was only a scattering of customers, a cluster of older men playing cards in one corner, three on-the-loose cowhands leaned against the bar, chatting.

'There's some fellas just rode into town,' Tonio called. 'From what I hear they're a hard bunch, quick to argue. They're looking for the Texan, Cal Jones. They got some kinda grudge aginst him.'

'Who hasn't?' A lanky cowboy, known as Kite, possibly because he was generally as high as one, grinned back at him. 'All power to their elbow.'

'The thing is,' Tonio said, standing halfway down the staircase, 'we don't want no trouble with 'em just yet. Don't let 'em rile ya up. In other words, keep outa their way. You understand?'

'Hoo!' Kite cheered. 'Why doncha put out the red carpet?'

Tonio descended to the bar, entwining his fingers, crackling the knuckles, nervously. He wondered whether he ought to send a rider to warn JayCee, but there wasn't time. Here they were, the gang of six men, pushing through the batwing doors, standing, getting their eyes accustomed to the gloom, checking the occupants. They were all hung with iron, and there was a menace about them.

'Welcome, gents,' Tonio called, strolling behind the bar. 'What's it to be?'

Houck led them across, their boots and spurs

clanking. He propped his carbine against the bar, removed his gloves and grunted, 'Whiskey.'

'Sure.' Tonio placed a bottle before them and arranged six tumblers. He filled each to the brim. 'You come far?'

'We sure have. We been riding fer ten days.' Houck had a deep, gravelly voice. 'You ever heard of El Paso?'

'Texas? That sure is a mighty long way.'

'Sure is.' Houck raised the glass in his fingers, rolled the fiery hooch around his mouth, and spat it out, angrily. 'What's this? Horse liniment?' He hurled the tumbler at a wall, smashing it, and growled, 'We want the best.'

Tonio started, nervously. 'Sorry. Most guys find this to their taste.'

Houck fixed him with his gimlet eyes. 'We're not most guys.'

'Right. Guess I'll have to give you JayCee's best bourbon. The finest there is. That OK?'

'Who's JayCee?' Houck demanded, his hands resting on the butts of his Remingtons, towering over Tonio.

'He's my father. He owns this joint. Most of the land around here, too. He's a big man in this valley.'

'His father,' Kite sniggered, looking along. 'His an' a hundred other little bastards, too.'

'All right, shut it,' Tonio snapped, 'or you can go fly your kite, Kite.' He took JayCee's bourbon from beneath the bar and a set of smaller glasses, carefully tipping the precious brew into each one. 'There y'are, gents. Good health.'

Houck held his arm as he went to remove the bottle. 'Leave that. An' bring out any more you got.'

'I, er. . . .' Tonio pulled at his lips, undecided. 'Yah.' He thumped another bottle of bourbon on the bar before them. 'That'll be ten dollars a bottle, twenty dollars.'

'Put it on the bill,' Houck growled, sampling it, daintily, a little pinky raised. 'Thass better.'

'This is OK fer me,' Funt giggled busy tackling the abandoned tumblers of red eye. 'Jest the job. I sure got me a thirst.'

'Me, too.' Schwarz was running fingers through his blond curls, his sweat-stained shirt sticking to his barrel-like girth. 'Gimme a beer. So, your so-called daddy owns the joint, does he? What else you got to offer here?'

'We got five very attractive young ladies upstairs. And by attractive, I mean attractive. They'd just suit you gents. Redhead, blonde, brunettes, they know all the tricks.'

'I bet they do. Like tryin' to relieve us of our wallets when we're roostered,' Ramirez, the 'breed, sneered. 'We can teach them a few tricks, too.' He slapped the quirt dangling from his wrist across the bar, viciously. 'Nuthin' I like better than to redden a li'l blonde gal's ass.'

The Mexican, Jorge, grinned evilly. 'Me, too.'

'Hey, gents,' Tonio protested. 'These are ladies.

They got class. They're not your two-bit whores.
We don't want none of that. You gotta treat 'em
nice, an' they'll be nice to you.'

'They'll get what they deserve.' The dark planes
of the part Comanche, part Mexican, part Texan
Jimmy Ramirez's face were set hard. 'They'll get a
little tickling. Thass what they'll get.'

The half-drunk cowboy Kite leaned over and
touched Houck's pigtail, giving it a gentle tug.
'Hey, whass this, tickle, tickle. . . .'

Ker-ash! The boom of Houck's right-hand
Remington shattered their ears as he turned fast
as a rattler, crashing out a shot through Kite's
chest. The foolish grin on the cowboy's face turned
to a rictus of agony as he lay on the floor, his arms
thrown back, a patch of blood beginning to blotch
his shirt.

'Nobody touches me,' Houck growled.

'Jeez!' Tonio gave a whistle as he watched the
blood begin to trickle across the stone floor. 'Well,
I did warn him. I'd better toss him out the back
'fore he messes the place up.'

'Don't make a move, cream puff. You got a
lawman in this town?' The smoking sixgun was
aimed in Tonio's direction now. 'Don't think you're
gonna sneak off an' warn him, no way.'

'The nearest lawman's at Duppa Springs an' he
ain't much use. But, we all saw it, didn't we, feilas?
It was a fair fight. Kite here shouldn't have pulled
this gent's . . . er . . . thang. That was provocation.
That would be too much for any man.'

The men muttered and returned to their cards, glad only that it was not their turn to go up against such *hombres*. Kite's two pals at the bar turned their backs and silently attacked their drinks.

'See,' Tonio smiled. 'Everybody agrees. It's not the sort of thing we care to happen in our establishment, but no need to worry—'

'Ah, shut up and throw him outside 'fore he bleeds all over the tiles,' Houck jeered, replacing his Remington.

When Tonio returned, the gunmen had settled themselves in JayCee's plush private booth, flipping the 'Reserved' sign away. JayCee won't take kindly to this, Tonio thought. But 'Give 'em anything they want', he'd said.

'You boys gonna eat first, or indulge yourselves upstairs?' he asked, going over to the table.

'We're looking for a fella called Jones, Cal Jones.'

'Jones, the sheepman? He's not the most popular person in these parts.'

'He ain't with *us*, either. You know where he is?'

'Yes . . . well . . . probably. I hear tell he's taken his sheep back up the mountain. He's got a kinda shack up at the top, a lean-to built against an overhang.'

'Can you take us to it?'

'Yes, I could, or show you the way. It's a good day's ride. Back the way you come in. You see the Mogollon Rim's like a half-horseshoe' – he scrawled a diagram in a pool of beer with his finger – 'here's Riba. You go up round the Rim gittin' higher an' higher until you reach his place. 'S'easy.'

'Right,' Houck growled. 'Less go.'

'What about the gals?' Tonio asked.

'Yuh,' Funt complained. 'What about the gals?'

'You'll have to wait,' Houck said, getting to his feet. 'There'll be plenty to celebrate, gals and whiskey, when we get back here.'

Funt watched Houck and the other outlaws swagger out of the saloon, gave a wink at Tonio, and leered, 'Would you believe he warned us not to cause no trouble and he goes an' plugs that guy fer pullin' his piggy tail? Thass something I allus wanted to do.'

'Well,' Tonio smiled, 'you know now you better not.'

'Hey.' Funt grinned green and back stubs of teeth at the two half-drunken cowpokes at the bar. 'Why don' you boys jine us on this sheepman hunt? More the merrier. It's gonna be fun.'

'Yeah, we all hate sheepmen,' one of them grinned. 'Maybe we will.'

Eight

'*Black, black is the colour of my true love's
hair. . . .*'

Cal had always loved singing, and his pleasant
deep tenor rolled out over the rocks and scrub of
the plateau, which stretched on up into the higher
altitudes of the Mogollon peaks, and beyond the
Matitzal and Sierra Ancha ranges. In winter they
would be covered in snow. A vastness, a silence, a
solitude. A man needed to sing, and when he was
in love, more so. He was still obsessed by
Margarita's image in his mind, by whether he
should stay, or go. Could he steel himself to try to
forget her, or even part from her for a year or two?
Could he cease thinking about her? Not to see her
made him feel as if he was torn apart physically.
It was as if he only came alive in her company.

They had moved the flock a good way along the
Rim, Cal on horseback, the Tonto on foot, slowly
urging them along. The sun was beginning to fall,
magnified by the heat-haze into a vast ball, signi-
fying what was soon to be the end of another day.

95

It was time to look for a place to camp. General
Crook, who had been in the lead, was obviously of
the same idea for he had dropped his bundle of
belongings amid a circle of stones and had caught
hold of a sheep who had lambed out of season. He
had her head behind him, her haunches between
his knees, and was kneading her teats, squirting
some of her precious milk into a clay olla. It would
be nice to have cream in their coffee for a change.
Cal had been carrying her lamb for a while over
his saddle horn, but he dropped him down gently
and the lamb ran bleating to his mother for his
share. The sheep weren't a lot of trouble at this
time of the year, just needed moving on to nibble
at what herbs and vegetation they could. They
were, of course, remarkably stupid critters, and if
one could get tangled in a thorn bush, or fall over
a cliff it would do so. Cal had just spent half an
hour cutting one free from a ditch of cactus it had
wriggled into. They were looking pretty emaci-
ated, but they had had a good drink when they
were down in the valley, and he guessed they
might survive. The real hard work for a sheepman
came at lambing time when he needed to be on
guard all night keeping the wolves and other
predators at bay. Then came the sheepshearing,
back-aching work, packing the wool and trans-
porting it in along the rocky trails to market.
There *was* a living to be made from sheep. If each
ewe had two lambs they could more than double
their herd. He had been thinking of trying to take

part of the flock over the mesa to Fort Apache to sell to the soldiers for slaughter, rather than risk going back down through the Basin.

Cal jumped down from Mosquito and set him free to forage for himself. He wouldn't roam far and by dawn would be nuzzling him, wanting his handful of grain. Cal collected some tinder-dry mesquite and quickly had a small fire going. He carefully rationed some water into their kettle and set to crushing coffee beans on a rock with the butt of his rifle. The Tonto, a man of middle years, gnarled and lithe by a life in the mountains, was an excellent shot with bow and arrow, the only weapon he carried, and had bagged a brace of partridge. He was squatting down plucking them for their supper. His dark face impassive, his long hair retained by a scarlet headband, he sat cross-legged, his muscled legs in the knee-length moccasins burned black by exposure to the sun. He had been named General Crook in honour of that wise soldier who had done so much to bring peace to this part of Arizona and who the Apache, themselves, called Grey Wolf. He had encouraged them to become self-sufficient sheepherders rather than warriors and had enrolled thirty-five Tontos as his scouts. It was their knowledge of Apache ways and terrain that had contributed to the defeat of the fierce Chiracahua band in the south, led by Cochise and, finally, his nephew, Geronimo. As the latter chief said, he did not mind fighting the Americans, but he could not fight his own people as well. Still, Geronimo and his men were in the dungeons of Florida now, and all their torture and terror had not done their people much good.

Cal sighed, pulled off his riding boots and put on a pair of light Comanche moccasins he had had since Texas. They were fine for sitting around the camp-fire at night. He supped his milky coffee and watched the sun begin its fall, as if it were bathing all this land in blood. Blood . . . blood . . . blood. He was tired of fighting and bloodshed. He had seen enough of it in the Rangers and had sworn he would never get involved willingly again. He had joined up as a lad of sixteen, when his mother had died, his sisters had married and his father was long dead. Perhaps he was looking for a family. The Texas Rangers had been set up initially to protect the frontier settlers from the ravages of the Comanches, but in the seventies it wasn't the Comanches they needed protection from, it was their fellow Texans, the wild ones, the murderers, thieves and robbers. No Texan felt a man unless he had a collection of guns and knew how to use them. And with no more Comanches to kill, the outlaws turned them on honest folk and each other. It was this gun culture, this outlaw instinct, fuelled by the availability of rough whiskey, that was a prime cause of the trouble. True, Texas had been in ruins after the war, but a man could still survive without going to the bad. Cal had had the notion that he could bring some peace and order to his territory and had helped bring in some very vicious criminals. He had noticed that a good many of the killings were racist in nature. The first man John Wesley Hardin shot, for instance, was a Negro, killed for no apparent reason. Hardin then killed the three soldiers sent to arrest him. The Rangers finally caught up with him in '77 and he was currently doing life in Huntsville, Texas. But, he wasn't the only one. Cal remembered as a boy in 1873 being taken by his mother to mingle with a crowd of more than a thousand people who had gathered in the open air outside Paris, Texas, to watch a black man called Henry Smith being hanged for allegedly raping a white woman, and the horror he felt at seeing the fellow scream and struggle as he was branded on the tongue before his neck was stretched. It was as if the Texans could not forgive the blacks for no longer being their slaves, for contributing to their defeat. All in all, it had contributed to his decision to get out, to head for Arizona, to start anew.

Cal stood up and wandered over to the cliff edge, a sheer drop of a thousand feet to wooded ravines below. He stared to the south, wondering where Margarita was, what she was doing, or thinking. 'She's out there somewhere,' he whispered, and began to sing again, another verse, singing as if his heart would burst, as if the song would reach out to her.

The Tonto was standing beside him. 'Who you sing?'

Cal touched his chest and threw his fingers fluttering out like a bird. 'To her with whom my heart is full,' he said. 'I'm lost in love.'

General Crook gave one of his rare smiles and tapped not his chest, but his loin cloth, gesturing a clenched fist. 'You want woman, huh?'

'Yes, I guess that, too. It's all part of it.' He slapped the Tonto on the shoulder and they went back to the fire. Crook didn't have much English, and Cal had yet to master the glottal stops and strange 'ss-ing' sounds of his language, so they conversed mainly by sign. Or Cal just rambled on hoping the Indian would understand.

'How's the cooking going?' he asked, sitting down again. 'I hope you don't mind my singing. The sheep don't seem to object. It must be my Welsh forebears. They came over the big sea by ship back in the forties. Coal miners. Caught gold fever, followed every stampede. Father backed the wrong side in the war and didn't come home. But we still carried on singing. They used to stand me on the kitchen table when I was a kid to listen to my pure soprano. The Jones boy. And here I am, still like some kid of fifteen who's kissed his first girl. Me, a grown man, who's seen all I've seen. Still, it's not unusual to be in love with somebody. Although I might think so, I'm not the first one. I bet you have been, too?' He tapped out a rhythm with his knife on the kettle and continued with his song.

*

'What the hell was that howling?' Jake Houck pulled in his bronc and stared up along the Rim through the fast encroaching dusk, as the last fiery portion of the sun slipped away.

'Sounds like somebody got bellyache,' Abel Funt whispered. 'Or mebbe it's the ghost of some 'pache. They say these hills is haunted.'

'Don't talk crap.' Schwarz sat his horse and his nostrils twitched. 'You smell what I smell? Supper roasting. It makes my belly rumble.'

'*Si,*' Jimmy Ramirez agreed, loosing a rattle of Spanish at his two Mexican pals. 'There's somebody along there.'

'What's that damn tinkling noise?' Jake asked, listening to the gentle tintinnabulation of sheep bells in the half-darkness.

'Sheep,' Tonio muttered. 'Can't you smell 'em? Maybe it's him. Well, I'll tell you one thing, I ain't losing another good hoss.' He jumped down and hitched his bronc to a bush. I'm goin' forward on foot.'

'Yeah, good thinkin',' Houck said. 'Come on, boys. We'll creep up on him, or whoever it is. I tol' ya we'd gotta keep goin'. This could be our lucky day.'

'Maybe our journey ain't been in vain,' Schwarz beamed, sliding from his exhausted bronc. 'I vote we take him alive. I want to see his face when he sees us. I want to have fun with this boy. I want to see him suffer the way we've suffered.'

'We gotta catch him first.' Houck eased the

Remingtons in his holsters. 'They're up along by the cliff apiece. We'll circle around, hem 'em in.'

The two 'punchers from the saloon dismounted, too, pulling carbines from their saddle boots. They were well whiskied-up and easily persuaded to join the 'posse' in pursuit of the lousy sheepman. They had ridden with the six *viciosos*, and Tonio, up along the Rim all day, the cliff edge on their left gradually rising higher and higher. They had just been debating whether to make camp and go on with their search in the morning.

'I'm sure damn glad he's quit that singing,' one of them giggled, taking a glug of whiskey from a bottle. 'It was making me feel queasy.'

'Yeah,' the other crowed. 'If there's a Tonto with him I want one of his ears.'

The nine men crouched low and spread out, dodging forward through the rocks, cursing silently as cactus snagged them, trying to edge through huddles of sheep without unduly disturbing them. In the still orange afterglow of dusk, Houck knelt and peered forward. He could see a thin spiral of smoke drifting from behind some boulders not far from the cliff edge. He grinned triumphantly, and beckoned with the flat of his hand to Ramirez and Raoul Garcia to push on up further. 'Now we got 'em cut off,' he gritted out to Schwarz, who was breathing heavily beside him. 'Ready?'

As he spoke, he saw the lanky Texan in Stetson and tattered chaps jump up onto a rock, silhouetted against the orange sky. He had a rifle in his hand and was looking around, as if he had heard something, probably the sudden clatter of sheep-bells as they dashed away from the men. 'He thinks there's a prairie fox sniffin' around,' Houck muttered, raising his right-hand Remington, taking careful aim at the Texan's upper thigh. He wanted to bring him down and, like Schwarz said, have his fun. 'I'll show him just what kinda fox I am.'

Suddenly, however, one of the half-drunken cowboys took a potshot at Cal with his carbine. The bullet cracked out, sending Cal's Stetson flying and whining away. 'Shee-it!' Cal gasped, slithering down by the fire. 'There's somebody out there trying to kill me. That was my best hat.' He reached out, studied the bullet hole, and jammed it back on. 'Maybe they didn't appreciate my singing.'

Houck was loudly cursing. 'You dang blazin' fool! I coulda got him then.'

A shiver ran down Cal's spine as he heard the raucous voice not thirty yards away and his eyes met those of the Tonto. 'I think I know who that is. Houck! What's he doing here?'

The answer came ringing through the air. 'I'm here to kill you, Jones. Remember me?'

'Shee-it!' Cal repeated, dumbfounded that a man could hold such a grudge. 'Whadda ya know?' He stood up and edged around the rock, peering across. 'Houck? I thought I had you locked up in jail for life. What you doing here?'

'I'm here to kill you. Don't you listen?' And a bullet chiselled rock by Cal's head. This initiated a veritable fusillade from all quarters around them. 'You're surrounded. You ain't git a chance in hell.'

'No.' Cal ducked back, leaning with his back to the rock, his heart thumping. At that moment it seemed that Houck was speaking sense. 'We're damn well surrounded.' He stared at General Crook, who was fitting an arrow to his bow. 'I don't think that's gonna be a lot of use against guns.' He reached into his saddle-bags and found his last box of a dozen bullets for the Creedmore. 'Nor are these. We used too dang many at the Snake Canyon battle.' He swallowed what saliva he had left. His mouth had gone dry. He stuffed the box of bullets in the pocket of his sheepskin jacket and levered one from the full magazine into the Creedmore's breech. 'Ready, *amigo*?'

The Tonto nodded and found himself a firing spot between two rocks. He pulled back the bowstring to full tension, watching alertly for one of the men to show himself.

'You still there, Jones? Or are you pissing your pants like a schoolgirl in a funk? Show yourself, you yellow-livered skunk, and fight.'

'If that's what you want, Houck.' Cal dodged to the other side of the rock, peered over, saw Houck and Schwarz, and pumped three fast shots at them, but they jumped down unscathed as bullets snarled around his own head from all sides. 'Phew!' he breathed out. 'Things are hotting up.'

He took off his Stetson, balanced it on his rifle barrel and poked it over the top. Bullets buzzed about it like bees and it was whipped away. Cal let out a scream and winked at the Tonto.

Houck, Schwarz and the others listened. 'We dang well got him,' one of the cowboys yelled, jumping forward over a rock. As he did so there was the hiss of an arrow and he hurtled back with it in his throat. His companion bent in horror to examine him, and another greasewood, semi-poisonous arrow thudded into his back.

Houck cursed some more as Ramirez yelled to him, 'There's a Tonto with him. He's got two of the boys.'

'That's just a start,' Cal yelled. 'If I were you I'd give up and go back to jail. You were nice and safe tucked up in ya bunks.'

'I don't give up.' Houck and Schwarz angrily loosed a hail of bullets at the Tonto, who jumped down, and rolled to another position. In the sudden silence, Houck shouted, 'Every day in that stinking jail you put me in I been thinking of this, Ranger, thinking of the day I'd get you. You got a couple of drunken cowboys, but there's seven more of us. The day has come, Ranger. You're gonna die.'

'You talk too much,' Cal shouted, and levered the Creedmore, aiming for the flashes of fire from a clump of cactus where the Mexicans were holed up. He managed to demolish the cactus, but he wasn't sure about the men, and had to pull into cover as another fusillade chiselled past him. Too close for comfort. Blood was trickling from his cheek. The Tonto had wriggled away to another position and was shooting his arrows, but the men ringing them had gotten cautious.

'We can wait all night,' Houck shouted, wishing that he'd thought to bring some dynamite.

'Waal, we cain't make a break 'cause we ain't got no dang horses,' Cal said to the Tonto, as he reloaded and tossed the empty box away. When he returned to a firing position he found that his assailants had closed in and he was capable of taking only wild shots between dodging back from their vicious attacks. He glimpsed a little guy in a top hat scrambling over a rock and blasted at him with the heavy Creedmore. There was a squeal, but Funt hopped away.

'Hey, *gringo*,' Ramirez shouted, gloatingly. 'Remember me? You running short of ammunition, huh? Soon we get you. Then I goin' to cut your balls off, eat them for my supper.'

Eight slugs left. Cal sent one in Ramirez's direction, hoping for a lucky shot. Seven. Every shot he fired brought five or six in reply. Another Mexican in a sombrero, Jorge, showed himself, leaping closer. 'Unh!' He collapsed back against a boulder as Cal's bullet tore into his chest. 'Well, there's one for the pot.' Six cartridges left. He levered another into the breech.

'Hey, Cal, how you enjoyin' yourself?' Tonio called. 'It was me showed 'em the way. You're gonna regret you ever came to Arizona. You wan' me to give any farewell message to the gal? She sure is some looker, ain't she? You know, maybe I'll have her myself. . . .'

He started into the sordid details of what he intended to do to Margarita. Angrily, Cal showed himself, and fired wildly Tonio's way. It was a fool thing to do. Bullets hurtled in reply, one tearing through his jacket at the shoulder. He wasn't sure if it had done any damage. Three slugs left. He slumped back behind the rock, staring at the fire. Maybe he should keep one for himself? The Tonto had one last arrow left. 'What we gonna do, *amigo*? Sorry to get you into this.'

'Come.' General Crook, serious-faced, beckoned his palm. 'It only chance.' He turned and knelt like a runner at the blocks and dashed in a beeline for the cliff-edge. He stood for a second and dropped down.

'Hey, you see that?' Funt shouted. 'The Injun went over the edge. He damn well committed suicide.'

That was the impression Cal had, too. Hell, why not? He clutched his rifle and ran as fast as he could. Bullets cut about him, but he reached the cliff and hesitated, looking down. There seemed to be some sort of ledge; General Crook was down there, beckoning. Cal dropped as close to the rock as he could. He hit the ledge and rolled. The Tonto

grabbed hold of him, a thousand-foot drop loom-
ing in the gloom beneath them. 'Jees-is!' Cal
gasped.

There were shouts up above as Houck and his
men came to peer over. Cal levered his rifle and
aimed upwards.

'Aaagh!' There was a scream as the horsethief,
Garcia, went twisting and turning like some
lunatic diver down through the darkness. He hit
bottom and the screams ceased.

'Come,' the Tonto hissed.

He clung to the side of the cliff, easing himself
along a fault, like a fly on a wall. Cal swallowed
his fear, slung the rifle across his back and
followed him. He was glad he had changed into
moccasins; he would have had no chance in heavy
boots. The men up above had started firing down,
trying to dislodge them, and he had to concentrate
hard, just follow the General. In the poor light any
slip could have been fatal, but the Tonto led him
on, reaching out a hand at a particularly treacherous corner to pull him into safety. After that it
was easier and they went leaping and hopping
down from rock to rock until they finally reached
the bank of shale at the bottom and skied down
through it to a ravine filled with trees. A bullet
whistled harmlessly by them, its report echoing
along the ravine. Cal turned and waved to the
tiny figures at the top.

'Too bad,' he shouted, gleefully, 'try again!'

General Crook tugged him by his jacket and he

followed him, running away through the dark trees.

'What's the hurry?' Cal panted. 'They ain't gonna follow us here.'

'This wood bad,' the General said. 'Ghosts.'

'Aw, yeah. I forgot.'

Nine

It was four on Sunday afternoon when Cortez raced his mustang into the ranch and found JayCee Lanchester working in the wagon-shed with Velasquez, helping fix a new iron rim to a wheel of the chuck-wagon. 'We showed that Texan a thang or two, you wouldn't believe it,' he blabbed out.

Excitedly, he described the gunfight, the deaths by arrow, the escape by leaping over the precipice, and how Jones had shot the two Mexicans.

'You mean you had 'em surrounded, nine men to two, and they outshot and outwitted you?'

'We got our own back this morning. We drove another five hundred of his sheep over the cliff. You shoulda seen 'em go cascading down. A great bloody pile at the bottom. That should put him out of business for good.'

'You damn fool,' Lanchester spat out, as he gripped tongs to hold the red-hot rim sizzling in a tub of water. 'We've nuthin' against him having his sheep up at the top; it's down in the valley we don't want 'em.'

'It weren't my idea,' Tonio replied. 'It's them other four. They're crazy for revenge.'

'You know,' JayCee said, his grey eyes serious, 'I'm almost beginning to feel sorry for this Texan. He's the only man among us with any guts.'

'I wouldn't feel sorry for him, JayCee. He's finished now. He must be out of ammo. That's why he made a break. He won't dare come back down into the Basin.'

'What about these other four varmints? What are they up to?'

'The news ain't too good on them. That's what I've come to tell you, JayCee. They're liquored up and wrecking the saloon, smashing the bottles and the furniture, and hurrahing the town. I told ya they killed Kite, that's the last time he'll fly. I paid to have him planted. Now they're using up all your best bourbon an' abusing the gals, and it don't look like they intend to pay a cent.'

'Abusing the girls?'

'Yeah. Beating-up on 'em. The Spanish woman took her daughter home. They never do it on a Sunday, anyway, and she didn't like the look of these four. The Latinos are locked and shuttered up and most the rest of the town's dumbstruck. What we gonna do, JayCee? Shall I break out the carbines and get the boys ready to ride?'

Lanchester held the rim, unspeaking, until Velasquez had hammered home his nails. 'Nope, I don't want to lose half my men in a shooting match, not with the round-up coming. These four are dyed-in-the-wool gunslingers. We gotta use cunning against 'em. First we gotta get 'em off our doorstep and outa Riba. I'll take care of this. You stay here, keep your eye on Margarita, make sure she don't leave the spread.'

'Where is she?'

'She's in the garden picking peaches. I forbade her to go into church today.'

'Right, I'll stay with her. But, JayCee, you take care. That Jake Houck's as crazy as a shithouse rat. They all are.'

'I can handle things,' JayCee said, grimly, as he went to sling his big Denver saddle on his quarter horse. 'I used to spit out men like them for breakfast.' He firmed on the cinch and tightened the latigo strap. 'Go get me my Colt. It's in my desk drawer.'

When Tonio returned with the nickel-plated .45 in its tooled leather gunbelt, his father took it, buckled it on under his suit jacket. He spun the horn-handled Colt's cylinder to check it was fully loaded and jammed it in the holster. 'Right, if I ain't back in four hours you better come looking for me.' He swung into the saddle and rode fast out of the barn door.

Cortez watched him go at a mile-eating lope, pounding away across the dried grass, and flashed a smile at Velasquez. 'I knew if I told him they were drinking his bourbon that would get him riled up.'

*

They had kept on walking through the night following a shallow stream that wound through thick timber, mostly pines, dark and gloomy as a cave. Cal Jones would have rested, but General Crook seemed intent on getting out of these dense woods, springing forward on his strong, rock-climber's legs, splashing through the stream glimmering in the moonlight. As the upper heights of the Mogollon Rim towering over them began to be flushed by dawn's rays they came out into a natural amphitheatre, shrouded by wild vines hanging from the trees, but they could see caves, or dwelling places carved out in its sides, like the Navajo pueblos further north.

'This musta been a prosperous village sometime,' Cal called, as he climbed up to one of the rooms, nosing inside its shady interior. There was the remains of a fire and shards of clay pots and, as he explored up higher, poked away in a corner he found an iron breastplate. The dry air in the chamber appeared to have kept it rust free. He poked it out with his rifle barrel to make sure there were no rattlers coiled inside, and waved it out of the cave doorway to the Tonto down below. 'Look what I found.'

General Crook did not look very impressed, obviously in a hurry to get away from this place where evil spirits lurked. And Cal, himself, found the oppressive silence of the place decidedly

creepy. 'I reckon the Spanish conquistadors musta
come through here. It's on the direct line of march
of Coronado upon Cibola on his expedition
through Arizona in 1541. They probably put the
village to the sword and took over this place. I'm
gonna hang on to this,' he said. 'It's got historic
value.'

The Tonto tugged at his sleeve. 'Come,' he
hissed, urgently.

'OK, OK, don't git agitated.' They padded on
their way, heading north upstream, pausing only
to pick wild plums and strawberries for their
breakfast. Before they reached the Tilburys'
place, the General pointed to a narrow goatpath
that would lead them to the Rim. By noon they
were back at their lean-to and found Mosquito
standing by their pack mule, Malaria, who gave
an indignant bray on seeing them.

'Mosquito musta wandered back on his own,'
Cal said, and went to see if there was any water
left in their barrel. He found it split open, the
staves punched in. Their few belongings in the
lean-to, the stove and clay jugs, had been thrown
about and smashed. 'Looks like they searched the
place,' Cal said.

There was a shrill whistle from up in the rocks
and old Randy came jogging down the slope on his
shaggy pinto. 'Hey,' he called. 'I hid in the rocks
when I saw them. I thought they'd killed ya. You
see what they done?'

'No, what?'

'The lousy bastards run that five hundred head you had with ya over the precipice.'

Cal stood as if stunned for moments, shaking his head. 'Those four are beginning to git me mad.'

'There were five of 'em. That young fella in black, Cortez, was with 'em.'

'I wonder,' Cal said, 'if he was acting on Lanchester's instructions?'

He went to the back of the more-or-less demolished lean-to and dug into the dirt with his fingers, pulling out the old Texas Paterson in its velvet cloth. He slid it into the pocket of his chaps, and patted it. There was something else metallic in the velvet, a shiny badge. He pinned it on his shirt. 'This is Ranger business.'

'I thought you'd resigned.'

'I'm on their reserve call-up and I'm temporarily re-enlisting. I got one slug in the Creedmore and six in the revolver. I'm gonna have to be very careful about picking my shots.'

'They're desperate men. They'll kill ya, Cal.'

'Maybe they will, maybe they won't. Which way they headed?'

'Back to Riba.'

'Right. We got nearly a thousand head of sheep left. You and General Crook herd 'em on further along the northern Rim. We don't want nobody gittin' at them. He put the wooden mule saddle on Mosquito, and slung a long leg over, turning him back towards the valley. 'So long,' he called.

Margarita saw her father go charging away across the plain as she came from the kitchen garden, a basket filled with sun-ripened peaches and apricots in her hands. From the blazing heat of the enclosed garden she entered the gloom of the hacienda, its five-foot thick adobe walls keeping it as cold as a dungeon in summer. Her father had decorated the walls with Indian weapons and curios, and in one corner was his big desk and swivel chair. Margarita sat at the table, selected a peach, washed and peeled it, and sank her teeth into its luscious flesh. She noticed that the desk drawers were opened and disturbed where Tonio had searched for their father's gun, and caught sight of the letter and Wanted bills from Texas. Normally, the very thought of prying into somebody's else's mail would have appalled her, but her curiosity was aroused. She hesitated awhile, but the impulse was too strong. She went over and perused the letter, her heart quickening.

'I thought so,' she cried, triumphantly. 'I knew he couldn't be a bad man.' And then she read the postscript and studied the posters. 'Oh, my God!' she whispered. 'I've got to warn him.'

Margarita grabbed her straw hat and shawl and ran out to the stables. Velasquez was not around, so she took the young filly from a stall and backed her into the shafts of the high-wheeled buggy. She found the appropriate harness and hooked it to the shafts, soothing the horse as she fitted the collar and bridle. Suddenly a man's hands caught hold of her around the waist, and she jumped, and tried to struggle free.

'Where do you think you're going?' Tonio hissed in her ear, his hands groping upwards beneath her loose blouse. He had hold of her from behind, pressing himself hard into her soft flesh. 'Ah, yes,' he sighed. 'Very nice.'

'Let me go!' she gasped. 'How dare you? JayCee will kill you.'

'JayCee's gone, and in my opinion he won't be coming back. He's getting old. He don't realize what he's up against. Those *hombres* are fast. And the same goes for your sheep-poke pal, Cal. He ain't got a chance. So that just leaves you and me, don't it, sweetheart?'

Margarita could feel his tongue licking nause-atingly into her ear as he held her tight and rubbed himself back and forth against her buttocks. His fingers had reached her breasts and were toying with the nipples.

'Howya like that, Margarita?' he groaned. 'I bet you love it, doncha? I can do more for you, girl, than that Texan.'

'Stop it!' There was a shrill fear in her voice as she struggled to get free, but he had hold of her hard and swung her to fall face down onto a pile of hay. 'I've got to go to him. I've got to warn him.'

'Aw, he knows what he's got coming.' Tonio laughed softly as he inserted a knee between her thighs. 'And, I think so do you, eh baby, know what you've got coming? I'm only doing what Daddy ordered, keeping you at home. Tell me, Margarita, has JayCee ever done it to you? Sometimes I get the impression.'

'Get off me,' she sobbed, as he held her face down in the straw, one strong hand gripping her wrists behind her, the other hoicking up her long skirt. 'How can you be so disgusting? He's my father for God's sake. You're my brother.'

'Only your half-brother,' Tonio drooled. 'That don't mean nuthin' in these parts. Go on, struggle, you stuck-up bitch. The more you struggle the better I like it. I been thinking about this a long time. You know what, I'm gonna give you a kid, an' we'll sell this place and go away together, somewhere no one knows us.'

'You're crazy!' she shrieked. 'No, please, don't do this.'

Tonio pulled off his leather belt and tied her wrists behind her. He had her by the hair and was reared up over her, giggling as he fumbled to undo his pants.

Suddenly a milk pail clanged against his head, the hard blow knocking him unconscious, and he slumped heavily upon her. Margarita struggled free and looked up to see the old groom, Velasquez, standing there, the heavy pail raised for a second blow.

'Thank God you came,' Margarita breathed out, rolling over, her skirt up over her thighs. 'I don't know why – it was like he went berserk.'

'Men sometimes do go crazy,' Velasquez smiled,

'when they see legs like those.'

'I've given him no – he's just spiteful and jealous of me.' Margarita straightened her underclothes and skirt, brushed straw from her hair. 'Is he dead?'

'No, but he'll have a thumping headache when he comes round. Don't tell him it was me, *señorita*. He would not hesitate to kill *me*.'

'Not if I take this.' She rolled Tonio over and unbuckled his gunbelt with its silver engraved Smith & Wesson .44. 'And if I lock up the armoury, he'll be a toothless dog that can't bite. Maybe it would be best, too, if you roped him to that post. I've got to go.'

'But Señorita Margarita you cannot go. Please no. Señor JayCee, he will fire me. He told me, it is not safe for you.'

'I don't care,' she said, strapping on the heavy gun. 'Somebody's got to do something for Cal.'

She paused only to lock up the house and the armoury, hiding the keys, and returned to jump on the rig, picking up the light whip. 'Don't worry, Velasquez, I won't let JayCee sack you. He will reward you for saving me.' Margarita tossed back her hair, and manoeuvred the buggy out of the wagon-shed, driving around the house and through the ranch gates, getting the feel of the reins, and then she set the filly off at a frantic high-stepping trot towards Duppa Springs.

When JayCee Lanchester rode into Riba the town

was deathly quiet. The townsfolk skulked behind their barred windows and shutters. Some men, storekeepers and tradesmen, had ushered their families indoors, and primed their rifles and shotguns for self-protection. But, so far, the *renegados* had only shot one drunken cowboy, Kite, which, some would say, was by way of doing the community a service. They had ridden up and down, shooting at signs, smashing windows, and yelling like Apaches. But hard men had to have their fun, and it was rumoured they had come to kill the Texan sheepman. So, the townspeople saw little reason to intervene. The *bandidos* were currently kicking up a stink along at the Red Rays saloon, and there was some dreadful language and caterwauling coming from windows upstairs. But if a woman was depraved enough to work in a place like that she should expect her just deserts. She could hardly expect to be treated like a lady. She had to reap what she sowed, take the good with the bad. That was what the good citizens of Riba reckoned, and they were relieved when they saw JayCee ride in. He was the owner of the saloon. It was up to him to sort matters out.

A shrill scream pierced the air from the open window of the bordello as Lanchester hitched his quarter horse to a rail. He frowned, pulled his suit jacket back to loosen his Colt in the holster, stepped up onto the sidewalk and into the saloon. The warning from Tonio had not prepared him for the full shock of the disaster inside: chairs and tables smashed, the big mirror behind the bar in broken shards, a chandelier in smithereens, bottle glass crunching beneath his boots, the faro table overturned, food from the kitchen plastering the walls, the place devastated and deserted.

'It looks like it's been hit by a tornado,' JayCee muttered as he went behind the bar to give himself a stiffener, but found his shelf of best bourbon bare.

If the four *viciosos* had returned to Riba at noon they must have had quite a lunchtime session. They had, apparently, slumbered through the afternoon until the effects of the corn and potato lightning wore off, and were now on the rampage upstairs. He could hear them thumping about, their loud, bullying laughter, the girls' squeals of fear.

'Maybe I made a mistake. I should have brought reinforcements,' JayCee muttered, as he tried to drink the remains of some rotgut from a half-broken bottle. He was bitterly aware that none of the townspeople had offered their aid. He had done them plenty of favours in the past. He suddenly felt somewhat old and foolish. Fortune, he knew, favoured the young and the brave. 'This ain't like fighting the Apache. This is a different kettle of fish.'

He tossed the last of the liquor down, made a grimace of distaste, braced himself, and strode, determinedly, up the staircase. It was odd how the older and richer a man got the more he was inclined to hang onto life. Yes, he was scared, fear fluttering inside. It was a new experience for JayCee.

'Satan certainly has no unemployment problems here,' he said, as he stood in the doorway and watched something akin to a scene from a Roman orgy. Jimmy Ramirez had his riding quirt of woven rawhide ending in four knotted tails gripped in his hand and was slashing it across the bare backside of LuluBelle, the crimson weals beginning to trickle blood as she yowled. JayCee was tempted to start shooting while they were off-guard, but, instead, yelled, 'All right, boys. That ain't no way to treat a lady. Let's call it a day, shall we?'

'Who the hail's the smartass?' Jake Houck was sprawled on an armchair, one hand holding a bottle, the other around the throat of the big-busted redhead, Rosemary. Her cheek was bruised, blood trickled from her swollen lips, and her green eyes were dazed. Her shiny, striped basque had been torn apart. 'You lookin' fer trouble, mistuh?'

The scrawny Kentucky Melanie was practically naked, her hair awry, as the burly German, Schwarz, laughter booming from his mammoth chest, smacked her backside and urged her on. 'JayCee, for Gawd's sake, do somethang!' she begged.

'JayCee?' Houck's fingers moved from Rosemary's throat, and flickered towards his gunbelt and twin Remingtons slung over the back of the armchair. 'Say, ain't you that rancher we heard about?'

'I own this joint. And I don't like what you're doing to it. Or to my girls. You've had your fun, boys. It's all on the house. I ain't gonna charge you nuthin', not for the damage to my furniture, nor for my liquor, nor the girls. You came to get Cal Jones, so I suggest you go finish what you came to do, and go on your way.'

'Listen to the banty li'l rooster,' Houck guffawed. 'He's got a nerve, I'll give him that. He's been sitting on this li'l dungheap in the back of nowhere so long he really thinks he's cock of the walk. I got another think comin' fer you, mistuh. Git lost. We ain't finished here yet.'

'Listen, boys, it's Sunday, and the store's closed,' Lanchester drawled, his voice tense. 'You better go look for Jones, 'fore he comes looking for you.'

'Jones? Huh!' Schwartz exploded with more laughter. 'We ain't worried about that dumb Ranger. He's as good as dead.'

'Be reasonable, boys,' Lanchester pleaded. 'Those girls look like they been run over by a stampede. Give 'em a break.'

Out of the corner of his eye, Lanchester saw Ramirez going for his shoulder-hung revolver and pulled out his Colt. But his instincts were not so spring coiled as they once had been. His Colt .45 was barely free of his holster, snagged by his jacket, when he heard two ear-shattering blasts, saw a plume of smoke coming from the 'breed's piece and felt like he'd been hit in the chest by a hammer. Simultaneously, Houck's Remington belched flame and lead and he felt the slug crashing through the flesh and bone, nerves and muscles of his leg. In spite of the excruciating pain, he tried to fire his revolver, but it fell from his fingers. He collapsed to the floor, one hand trying to staunch the blood from his chest, the other nursing his shattered knee. As he lay there, the men's grinning faces wavered back and forth in a haze of gunsmoke. This is it, he thought. Go on, finish me. But the third expected shot did not come.

'Maybe the peanut's got a point,' Houck said, tossing Rosemary aside as he got to his feet and slung his gunbelt over his shoulder. 'Maybe it's time to make tracks. I ain't gonna miss the chance of gittin' Jones.'

Ramirez grinned and gave LuluBelle a last slash with his quirt for luck and stumbled out after Houck. The burly German grabbed his hat, picked up his carbine, and booted Lanchester in the gut as he stood over him. "Bye 'bye, mistuh. That'll teach you not to poke your nose where it ain't wanted. ''Bye 'bye, gals. Have a good day.'

The girls slowly groped their way upright, as if they could hardly believe their ordeal was over. 'Hey, look at JayCee,' Melanie drawled. 'Somebody better go get Doc Barnett.'

'Or,' said Rosemary, 'O'Farrell's Funeral Services. I thank he's day-ed.'

Ten

Margarita had the filly going at a steady trot
along the dirt road towards Duppa Springs when
she felt some plinks of cold water brushing her
face. For moments she couldn't think what it was,
it had been so long since they had had rain, and
the sky was clear, turning peach-coloured as the
sun began its fall. But, boiling up behind the
Mogollon range, were bruised clouds, travelling
fast, suddenly blotting out the sun. A cool down-
draught from the mountains must have carried
the droplets of water with it. What a relief! The
rains at last! The water was refreshing on her
skin. But then came an ominous rumble, and a
crack of thunder that sounded as if it was tearing
the earth apart. The clouds had turned the colour
of gunmetal, casting a dark shadow over the
Tonto Basin, and the drizzle began to intensify.
'Wait for the lighting,' she whispered, and there it
was, a forked streak of it daggering into the
prairie, making the filly miss her stride, toss her
head, and give a shrill whinny of fear.

125

Margarita hesitated, considering pulling in, putting on her waterproof woven Navajo poncho, sheltering until the storm had passed, but she heard another crackling sound coming from behind her, and shrill yips. She looked back and saw four men galloping across the prairie, quirting their horses, and firing their revolvers. At first she thought they might be some of her father's ranch hands sent to bring her back. But, no. 'They're firing at us,' she cried to the filly, alarmed, as a bullet snarled past her head. She could hardly believe it. It had never happened to her before. 'Jesus, Mary and Joseph!' she gritted out, slashing the whip across the filly's back. 'Yaugh! Go!' The filly skittered away at full pelt, and Margarita crouched over the reins, balanced on the bouncing buggy, urging her on. Through her mind flashed the memory of four faces on the Wanted posters; evil, vicious faces, and the details of their misdemeanours – robbery, homicide, rape. . . . 'God help me!' she cried, whipping harder, racing along the trail. 'Go! Go!'

Fat raindrops began to splatter into her face, her eyes, almost blinding her, but she hung on, careering along the dust track. There was another vast drumroll of thunder, and an ultraviolet blob of lightning fizzled past her, scorching the ground. The gunshots from behind were getting closer, louder, and a bullet splintered the buggy's footboard. Margarita glanced back and saw the four men pounding along the track, yelling and whooping, gradually reducing her lead. Frantically, she pulled out the Smith & Wesson and fired back wildly, but it was difficult to hold the heavy self-cocker steady, and her father had forbidden her taking lessons in firearms, so her shots went wild. As she leaned back, she inadvertently pulled on her left-hand rein, confusing the filly, who was startled by another great flash of lightning that cleaved a cottonwood tree and filled the air with a stench of burning. Her hooves flying, the horse veered off the track, sending the buggy bouncing. The traces were cracking apart, and the rig was turned on its sidewheels, gradually, with the certainty of fate, about to crash over on its side. Margarita stared at the ground coming closer, petrified, hanging on, then hurled herself out, and rolled free into the thick grass. The fall knocked the wind from her body, but, gasping for air, she hung onto the Smith & Wesson and, as a horseman loomed up over her, squeezed the trigger again, aiming to kill. The slug sent his hat flying to reveal a shaven head, thick silver rings in pointed ears. His thin lips opened in a leer, and he laughed, gutturally, pulling his horse to one side as she fired again, and missed. He leaped from the saddle and kicked a boot at her chin, toppling her backwards, ripping the revolver from her fingers.

'Hey,' he said, examining the silver-enscrolled weapon. 'A nice piece. Just as well she don't know how to use it.'

Margarita was sitting up, feeling her aching

jaw as the rain streamed down her face, and the
thunder rumbled its vast drumrolls down from
the mountains. Dread filled her as she met the
eyes of the four men watching her gloatingly.

'You had better not touch me,' she warned them
severely. 'My father is JayCee Lanchester. He
ranches this valley. He will hunt you down and
hang you.'

'Heck! He'll be durned clever if he kin do that.'
A hunched-up little man in a top hat and over-
large topcoat leaned on his saddle horn and
grinned at her. 'He's day-ed. We kilt him.'

'Yeah,' Houck snarled, kneeling down and
chucking his forefinger under her chin. 'We're
takin' over this valley. Did I hurt you, pretty gal?
That ain't nuthin' to what I'm gonna do.'

'Hey, what a beaut! Look at that lily-white
skin,' Schwarz bellowed. 'I'm gonna have a jolly
ride on *her*.'

'*Si*,' Ramirez agreed, slapping his quirt against
the leather of his leg. 'We gonna have a party.'

'Not until after I'm done,' Houck shouted, and
he knelt down over her as, her hair and blouse
sodden by the rain, she tried to back away, a look
of horror on her face as his thick fingers crudely
fondled her. He stuck the barrel of the S & W
under her chin and grinned as he squeezed the
trigger. The hammer clicked home. The cylinder
was empty. How, she wondered, had he known? Or
didn't he care? She almost wished the gun had
been loaded. 'Funt, go and catch that filly of her'n.

We're gonna take her with us,' Houck was saying, and she gasped a prayer of relief for the reprieve. The rain was tumbling down in sheets, darkening the land, and he was doubtless sated by his afternoon activities. 'She'll keep,' he shouted. 'Nobody touches her 'til after me.'

He hauled the girl to her feet and fixed his lariat noose around her neck, jerking it tight. 'Git on that hoss. You're coming with us.'

The stunted man in his ragged macinaw had returned with the filly and Margarita was forced at gunpoint to jump on her bareback. She had never ridden astraddle before, or side-saddle come to that, so she just hung onto its coarse mane and tried to go with its jogging rhythm.

'Hey, this gal's a Godsend,' Houck yelled through the storm. 'Didn't that jumped up li'l fart, Tonio, say that Ranger Jones was crazy as a loon fer JayCee's daughter? She's gonna be our ace. We can use her to lure him in.'

Margarita was dragged along by the rawhide cord tight around her throat, trying to keep up, drenched and miserable, as they headed along the now muddy trail to Duppa Springs. All she could hope was that one of the sizzling bolts of lightning might hit their iron weapons or bridles. But that would be asking too much of God.

Like many fat men, Sheriff Alfie Polanski was a cheerful, easy-going character, and there was nothing he liked better when night fell than to sit

on the sidewalk outside his office and play his big
banjo. There would often be a little crowd of children and onlookers gathered round jigging their
toes as the sheriff, his several chins beaming and
bouncing, entertained them. He was renowned as
a mean banjo-plucker. The fact that it was pouring cats and dogs, as the mysterious saying goes,
did not deter him that night. All the more reason
to celebrate. The longed for summer rains had
finally arrived. The only concession he made was
to sit just inside his office doorway so he didn't get
too wet and tonight he played, of course, without
an audience; they were all in their homes, or the
saloon, taking refuge from the heavy rain and
flashing storm. The sound of the thunder was so
tremendous he could hardly hear his own music,
and so engrossed was he in his fingerwork that he
did not notice four horsemen who came riding
along the churned-up main street of Duppa
Springs, followed by a bedraggled girl riding bareback.

'Well, bless my soul, just look who's there,'
Houck grinned, as water tipped from the brim of
his hat. 'A guardian of the law. don't you just love
him, boys? What's he doin' the dingbat?'

'He ain't see'd us,' Funt giggled. 'He's havin'
hisself a concert.'

'Git up on the roof, Abel.' Houck winked at him.
'You know what to do.'

The square-shaped adobe had a flat roof with a
fine crop of marigolds growing from it behind the

crude sign which announced, 'Town Jail'. Funt
rode his nag over to the side, nimbly stood up on
his wet saddle, grabbed hold of the top of the 'dobe
and hauled himself up. He had taken his lariat
with him and carefully tied it to the post of the
sign and spread out a noose in his hands.

'Hey, Sheriff.' Houck jerked his noose so that
the girl was pulled into the cover of his fellow
riders. 'We got bad news.'

Polanski looked up, surprised to see the three
mud-splattered men. He peered at them out in
the dark and wet, and stepped out onto the sidewalk beneath the swinging hurricane lamp.
'What's wrong, fellas?'

'There's a fella been shot back in Riba and a gal
kidnapped,' Houck roared.

The sheriff still had his banjo in his hands. He
couldn't see the men well, but he imagined they
must be 'punchers from down Riba way. He strode
out to get a better look at them. 'Step down, boys.'

'You got any deputies?' Houck asked.

'Nope. I'm in sole charge of Javapai County. I
ain't seen nuthin' suspicious—' His words broke
off into choked surprise as a noose dropped
around his arms, and they were hugged tight into
his body as little Abel Funt up above hauled on
the rope giving a shrill 'Yee-hoo!'

'We got ourselves a sheriff.' Jake Houck grinned
as he removed his hat and let the water sheen
down his shaven skull. 'Jest look at that fat pig.'

Polanski had dropped his banjo and was struggling to try to reach the .45 holstered on his hip as he swung back and forth. His smile had vanished as he listened to the coarse laughter. 'This your idea of a joke? Come on, cut me down, boys. That's enough of the horseplay.'

'*Mein Gott!*' Schwarz beamed. 'He really thinks we're joking. Ain't you heard of us, mister? We're the Houck gang.'

'Yeah.' Jake Houck rode forward, jumping his horse up onto the wooden sidewalk. He pistol-whipped the sheriff across his jaw and relieved him of his revolver, tossing it away into the mud. 'OK, Abel, cut him down.' As the sheriff landed with a thump, Houck ran his big horse into him, pushing him back, ducking through the door and running him back into his own office.

There was little the lawman could do but throw off the rope and raise his hands as Houck pointed the business end of a big Remington at him. 'You're making a big mistake, son.'

'Yeah, that's what my mama told me.' Houck spurred his horse, squeezing Polanski back against the bars of his cell. 'Toss me them keys on your belt. If you want to live, Sheriff, don't try nuthin'. I'm a compassionate man, but I don't take no for an answer.'

Polanski did as he was bid, passing the ring of keys to the outlaw. 'What you want here with us?'

'Well, for a start we might see what they got in the bank and the saloon.' He swung down and expertly frisked the sheriff, removing a knife from his boot. 'Get in.' He shoved him in his own cell and locked up, putting the keys in his coat pocket. 'But mainly we're here to arrange a reception for some Texan called Jones.'

'The sheepman?'

'Yeah, we got his gal outside. JayCee Lanchester's daughter. You know her?'

'Margarita? Of course I know her. You wouldn't harm her?'

'Harm her. Nah, of course not.' Houck cackled at the lawman's naivety. 'We're gonna, shall I say, re-educate her. She's gonna love what we do to her.'

Houck strolled out of the adobe, kicking the banjo aside, calling, 'So long, dumbcluck. We'll be in touch.'

The storm showed no sign of abating as he hauled Margarita from the horse and dragged her by the rope around her neck over to the town flag-pole in the centre of the muddy street. 'Here y'are.' He thrust her back against it and ran the rope round and round her body, jerking her bonds tight. 'You're going to be the bait, our sacrificial lamb to catch the tiger. Only Ranger Jones ain't much of a tiger these days.'

Jimmy Ramirez, in his big sombrero, grinned at her and gripped her face in his hand with the two fingers missing. She shuddered as she remem-bered his description – 'a man who favours cutting throats to shooting his victims. . . .'

'Hey,' Jimmy said, 'why don't we make her drop her panties and run them up the flagpost?'

'Great idea,' Houck growled, 'but we ain't got time. Come on, we gotta have a looksee at who's in this town. Round up any possible troublemakers.'

The four outlaws splashed through the heavy rain over to the town saloon where a dozen men were staring over the curtain rail out of the window at the downpour and the girl tied to the flagpole.

'What the hell you doin' to that gal?' one asked as Houck and his cronies clumped in.

'Waal, what a fine collection of drowned rats,' Houck grinned, and jabbed a finger at the thin, balding town barber, who had put the question. 'You got any objections, mister?'

The barber stared into Houck's muddy eyes and blanched. 'No-oh, I ain't. It's 'tween you and her, I guess.'

'You guess right.'

'He might not have any objection, but I have.' A dumpy, middle-aged man in range clothes, a small rancher, was standing by the bar patting the revolver in his holster. 'That's JayCee Lanchester's daughter. You ain't got no call to treat her like that.'

'Ain't I?' Houck turned to him, casually taking off his hat, slapping the rain off against his thigh, but using it to cover his left-fist which slid across and came out with the Remington from his right holster. *Ker-boom!* It spurted flame and death, catapulting the rancher back against the bar before he had his own weapon out. Blood flowered on his shirt and he slid down, gasping his last. 'Anybody else?' Houck asked.

As sulphurous gunsmoke drifted, the men in the saloon stood stunned, covered by the three other desperadoes, who had arranged themselves at convenient points and jerked out revolvers and carbines. 'No, I don't think these others got much to say,' Abel Funt hooted, and dodged about relieving them of their sidearms.

The barkeep made a surreptitious movement with his hands beneath the bar and Houck pointed the Remington at him and growled, 'Go on. Try me.'

The 'keep slowly raised his hands, and Abel went and found the sawn-off beneath the bar, tossing it onto the pile of hardware in the corner of the saloon. 'Right, that seems like everybody,' he giggled. 'What we gonna do with 'em, Jake?'

Houck tossed him the ring of keys and said, 'You three take 'em over to the jail and let 'em partake of the sheriff's hospitality in his cell. And round up any other stray men you see. We don't want nobody taking potshots at us when we're busy. Meanwhile, I'm gonna gargle a glass of this rum. You boys better not have any yet, you gotta stay sober.'

'Aw, Jake, that ain't fair,' Abel said. 'Just give us a bellywarmer.'

'Nope. You know what you're like,' Houck grunted. 'Once you start you cain't stop. Same goes for you, Jimmy.'

'Jake's the boss,' Schwarz boomed out. 'He's right. Once we're done there'll be plenty of time for boozing and' – he beamed and licked his lips – 'taking a ride on that li'l lady out there.'

They jabbed their weapons into the men, making them troop out like a line of convicts tramping through the mud to the jail, picking up a couple of other townsmen *en route*. There was standing room only in the barred cell by the time they had shoved them all in. 'Have fun, boys,' Funt giggled. '*We*'re gonna.'

When they emerged into the rain there was a shrill whistle and they saw Houck standing outside the bank. He beckoned them over with his revolver. Inside the dank, high-windowed building the banker, a Latino, and his teller, were unaware of events outside, apart from the fact it was raining.

'Good evening, gents,' the teller smiled. 'Well, not a good one, but it's good to have some rain. You cattlemen will be glad to see it, I guess.'

'Shut up, shortass. Find a coupla sacks and shove in it all the spare cash you got.' Houck brought the right-hand Remington up to the grille and aimed it at the teller's forehead. 'Pronto. And it ain' no use tryin' to contact the sheriff with any secret alarms. He's indisposed. We got this town tied up. So just don't argue if you aim to stay healthy.'

Jimmy Ramirez was rattling out a similar message in shrill Spanish at the dark-haired young banker, in his suit and bow-tie. The Latino looked crestfallen, but he nodded to the teller to do as they said. When the contents of the safe and bank drawers had been stuffed into the sacks, some thousands of dollars, the teller passed it through. 'There y'are, gents thass all there is.'

'Yee-hoo,' Funt warbled. 'We're rich.'

'Hand over the keys to the side door and front door,' Houck ordered, and the banker reluctantly did so. 'Right, you're locked in and you don't try to git out, savvy?'

'But what about my wife?' the teller protested. 'She's expecting me home to dinner. She'll be very annoyed if I'm not there.'

'He's more scared of his wife,' Houck grinned, 'than he is of me.'

'Ah, too bad,' Schwarz beamed. 'Give me your address and I will personally call and comfort her.'

'Oh, no, please, don't hurt her—' The teller gawped at the men as they sauntered out and slammed the front doors. He heard the key turn in the lock. 'Well, really!'

The Latino shrugged and said, 'They won't get far.'

'I don't know, sir,' the teller squeaked. 'They looked like professionals to me. I wonder what's going on out there.'

'We're probably better off in here,' the banker sighed, and his dark eyes rolled with alarm at two loud gunshots outside.

The town hog gelder, Hyram Watts, had been watching the mysterious goings-on in the main street from his slaughter house. He had reached for his big hog-killing gun as he saw the four men step out of the bank. They were carrying bags in their hands which they hadn't had with them when they went in. He had crept forward, waiting until they passed his shop, aiming for the big bald-headed man. But at the last moment, as he fired, he slipped on a mess of blood and mud and the blast from his weapon peppered the air. Houck made no similar mistake. He turned to the figure in the doorway and blasted him to Kingdom Come, leaving him collapsed in a tub of pig guts.

'You cain't trust nobody,' Houck growled, blowing down the barrel of his smoking revolver.

The rain streaming down his face, he looked across at the girl tied to the post and grinned. 'Abel, go ring the church bell. We want anybody else in town in the meeting hall, wimmin and kids, the lot.'

As Funt scampered away through the by now ankle-deep mud, Houck pushed through the front door of the town gunshop, illuminated by a hurricane lamp. The owner, Sam Zabriskie, was busy with his tools dismantling an ailing Winchester. 'What's all the commotion out there?' he called, looking up as his bell clanged.

'What the hell you think it is?' the curly-haired German grinned. 'We're robbing the bank.' He thrust a carbine in Zabriskie's face. 'You're a bit slow on the uptake, aincha, old man?'

'I was preoccupied,' Sam said, 'and my hearing ain't too hot these days. You say you been robbin' the bank? So, whadda ya want with me?'

'Half-a-dozen boxes of .44s,' Houck said. 'I'm gittin' low. Too many damn people have to argue with me.'

'Yeah.' Jimmy Ramirez opened the glass case to examine a nickel-plated Allen and Hopkins .36 boot gun. 'Hey, I like thees. I take it.'

'That's a fifty-dollar gun,' Zabriskie said. 'I'll throw in a box of .36s.'

'You'll do better than that,' Houck said. 'You'll hand me the contents of your till. I'm feeling greedy today. We need to git all we can 'fore we head for Colorado.'

'You durn cheatin' bastards, this is my livelihood.' Sam came up from behind the counter with a shotgun. Ker-pow! The bandits all ducked and hit the floor as the first blast of pellets shattered the shop windows. But Jimmy Ramirez made no mistake with the little .36 and it was Zabriskie who hurtled back to hit the deck before he could fire his second barrel.

'So long, sucker,' Schwarz smiled, putting a revolver to his temple to finish him. 'You just don't get nowhere being nice to people these days.'

'Hey, this wouldn't make a bad vantage point, right opposite the flagpole. Jimmy, you stay here and keep a watch out. You certainly won't run out of ammo,' Houck grinned. 'I'll send you over some

vittles from the saloon. There's firewood here. You
could light his stove, git your clothes dried. We
might have a long wait.'

'Aw, why do I get all the crappy jobs?' Ramirez
whined.

'Whadda ya mean? We gotta go plodding
around in the storm,' Houck said. 'We've a public
meeting to address.'

Funt was out in the street in the pouring rain,
his carbine in his hands, directing everybody, who
came running to see why the church bell was ringing, into the courthouse. He had ordered the
pastor to keep tolling on the bell on pain of meeting his Maker earlier than he had hoped if he
ceased.

The courthouse was half-filled with a steaming
damp mass of old men, women and children, both
Anglo and Mexican. Colonel Dangerfield had
appointed himself their leader and stood up as
Houck ambled in, followed by Schwarz and Funt
toting their guns. 'What the devil's the meaning of
this?' he demanded.

'Who the hell are you?' Houck muttered, darkly.

'Colonel Dangerfield. I act as coroner and
judge.'

'Well, Mistuh Coroner, you gonna have a few
more bodies to attend to. So, if you don't wish to
be in danger of being one yourself you'll shut up.
I ain't too fond of judges. They've wasted years of
my life. By the way, anybody here carrying a
hidden weapon had better surrender it, pronto.

You're all under house arrest. We got business in this town. You stay here all night, all of you, until our business is over.'

'I suppose I'd better give you this,' Dangerfield said, producing a two-shot derringer. 'I've seen what you do to those who argue. I will take responsibility to see these people give you no trouble, and I want your word that they will be unharmed.'

'You want my word? Don't go giving me orders, spindleshanks. It's me who gives the orders,' Houck glowered. 'We'll burn this town down if we've a mind to.'

'Calm down, man,' Dangerfield snapped. 'What is this business you have here?'

'OK, you'll all be OK.' Houck tried to quieten the whimpering women and children. 'You stay here you'll come to no harm. We're here to meet one man, Ranger Jones, the sheepman. We're gonna kill him and take his woman, and we'll be through.'

'You're crazy,' Dangerfield said. 'This is outrageous.'

'Don't you go calling me crazy, dumbhead.' Houck pointed a finger at him. 'Now, is there any youngster here knows where Jones hangs out? Here's a twenty-dollar bill for him if he rides through the storm to find Jones and tells him we're waiting.'

'Si, amigo,' a twelve-year-old Mexican boy, pushed forward by his mother, darted to the front and snatched the twenty-dollar greenback. 'I go. I have my burro. I know the trail. I not frightened of the storm.'

'Good kid. At last there's somebody in this town with some sense.' Houck tousled his black mop. 'There might be another twenty if you bring him in fast as you can. You just tell him Houck is here, he's got the Lanchester gal, and he's gonna do nasty things to her. *Comprende*?'

'Si, señor.' The boy saluted as if Houck might be a general. He gave the bill to his mother and dashed from the room. 'I get my burro.'

'Right, now you people just settle down. I don't want a squeak outta ya. I put you in charge, Colonel. We see anybody on the street, they git it same as Jones is gonna.'

Eleven

No man feels easy in a lightning storm, the possibility of instant, fizzling death, and Cal Jones was no exception, but he also felt elated as he guided Mosquito down the treacherous track from the Rim, now frothing and bubbling with a fierce stream. At least the desert would bloom and his, or Randy's, sheep, what few they had left, would put some flesh on their skeletal bones. But there was also an excitement about defying the elements, to see all about, beyond the saw-toothed *barrancas* and *cañons* of the distant mountain ranges, a flickering of vicious lightning stabs illuminating the purple ranges like stage settings in the night. There was an elation too, about putting his life on the line, not knowing whether he would live or die.

So, being elated, Jones sang as he rode. He was roaring a song at the top of his lung power like some madman, competing with the howling of the storm when in a sudden flash he saw a boy on a burro riding up through the stunted trees of Manzanita Canyon.

'Hello, there, boy,' he shouted. 'What brings you out on a night like this?'

The Mexican youngster smiled from beneath his straw hat, glad that his errand was completed without going too far. It was the easiest twenty dollars he had ever earned, in fact, a fortune in his eyes. '*Señor*, Houck has sent me to tell you he is waiting for you in Duppa Springs. He has Señorita Margarita roped to a pole in the main street and he say he do bad theengs to her eef you no come.'

At the mention of Margarita, Cal's face tensed. 'Is she all right, boy?'

'*Si*, I theenk so, but she does not look good. These *bandidos*, they have locked all men in jail and rest of us in courthouse.'

'How many of 'em are there?'

'Four, *señor*, I theenk.'

'A big, bald-headed one? A fat, blond German one? A 'breed with two fingers missing from his hand? And a little runt called Funt?'

'*Si, señor*. That is they.'

'Right, let's go. What's your name, son?'

'Emilio.'

'Well, Emilio, you're a brave kid to ride out in this storm. When we get to Duppa Springs you git back in the courthouse and take cover, you hear?'

'*Si, señor*. But is there not something I could do to help you?'

'Nope. I ain't sure there's a lot I can do to help myself.' Cal pursed his lips in a worried way as he rode through the canyon of ruddy-barked trees, with their thick green leaves, where once not long ago he had sat and held Rita in his arms and felt her lips against his own. 'All I can do is try. The odds don't look too good.'

He rode on and out of the canyon. It was not far to Duppa Springs now. The rain had eased to a steady drizzle. He licked the refreshing water from his lips and called to the boy on his trotting donkey. 'I don't suppose you noticed where any of these men had positioned himself?' He repeated the question in frontier Spanish when the boy looked puzzled.

'Ah, *si*. One I saw, the little one, climb to church belfry. The others I am not sure. Maybe one is in jail.'

'Waal, that's a help. Remind me, when I got any cash, to flip you a quarter.'

'Thass OK,' Emilio grinned. 'For you the information is free. You have come to save us.'

'That sounds kinda preposterous,' Cal grinned, 'but I'll try. I gotta be careful. I ain't got many bullets. And those boys got more twists than a barrel of snakes.'

Schwarz was taunting the prisoners jammed in the cell in the jailhouse. He jumped up and down, twanging the sheriff's banjo, roaring:

'I'm making my home in the hoosegow
'Til the moment they let me go free,
Oh, please send my mail to the hoosegow,
Let her live in my mem-em-or-reeeee!'

His chins wobbled with merriment at his own wit, and he called, 'What's the matter with you miserable sodbusters? I told you to sing the chorus.'

'We ain't got enough room to take a breath,' the sheriff complained.

'Ah, what a shame,' Schwarz cooed. 'Now you have a taste of what I and my friends have had to suffer on account of lawmen like you and Jones. You know what I'm going to do before I leave town? I'm gonna burn you all alive.' He struck a match on his thumb to give emphasis to his threat and tossed it into the waste basket which began to burn merrily.

Suddenly the church bell tolled and he turned to the barred window of the adobe jailhouse, poking his carbine through and peering into the gloom. Was he mistaken, or was that the Texan ambling slowly on his horse up the centre of the muddy street? 'It's the Ranger,' he hissed, resisting the desire to let loose a shot at him. He looked across the wide street to the gunshop on the other side. He could see Ramirez hovering in one of the windows. 'Steady, let him get closer,' he gritted out. 'Come, little fly, come into the spider's web.'

Jake Houck had doused all the lights in the saloon and stood looking across the top of the

batwing doors, his Remingtons in his hands. He
had seen the Texan coming, too. There was something odd about him. He was bulkier than he
remembered him, his sheepskin coat wrapped
tight around his chest. He blinked his eyes and
wished he hadn't had so many rums. The guy
was taking a big risk, wasn't he? In fact, suicidal.
He surely knew they were waiting for him. Once
he got close to the girl he would be in a crossfire
of four strategically placed guns. 'This time,
Jones,' he muttered, 'it's curtains for you. I'm
gonna git you, you see. There's no way you can
git outa this.'

To add insult to insolence, Ranger Jones
appeared to be singing as he made his way up the
street in the storm:

> *'When I was an apprentice*
> *I went to see my dear . . . .'*

'Go and rot in hell,' Houck roared, cocking his
right-hand Remington, sending a slug whistling
towards the sheepman. He was sure it hit him in
the chest for Jones recoiled backwards, almost but
not quite falling from his horse, which ploughed
around in the mud. 'What the hell?' He sent three
more shots whanging towards him, and the same
thing happened again. The rain had begun sheet-
ing down like arrows in his eyes and Houck could-
n't be sure of his target. He needed to get closer.

There was another rip of lightning, high and far

away across the mountains, a purple light brightening the whole valley and town even through the rain. Margarita screamed, struggling against her bonds, her face agonized, her black hair like snakes clinging to her high cheekbones, her cotton blouse plastered to her body and breasts so that the nipples were pressed against the material like stars. 'Cal, go back!' she shrieked. 'They'll kill you.'

Cal Jones had his Creedmore in his hands and, as the sky was lit by another violet flash, he swung it up towards the church steeple where a hunched man in a bulky coat was silhouetted against the sky, a carbine in his hands. Jones took careful aim with his one and only slug. *Pow!* Abel Funt threw up his arms and toppled from the tower, his coat billowing like a bat that couldn't fly. He hit the mud on his back, kicked up one leg and lay still.

The Texan silently thanked Emilio for warning him about the church tower, tossed the Creedmore away, swung from his horse, and looked around as he drew the Paterson from his chaps pocket. Flame erupted from the window of the gunshop as Jimmy Ramirez fanned his revolver, aiming like all professional shootists for a heart shot. Jones staggered back but did not go down. The 'breed, in his big sombrero, stared with horror as Jones slowly aimed the Paterson. The bullet pirouetted him, and he tumbled out of the window onto the sidewalk.

The sheepman turned to face the jailhouse and

the saloon, sending two shots crashing out to splinter the saloon batwing doors and making Houck dive for cover.

'That dumb, crazy bastard,' Schwarz bellowed, and began levering his carbine, sending bullets whistling through the rain. One hit, bull's-eye! Right in the heart. And Jones was knocked backwards to land in the mud. 'Got him!' Schwarz turned to the men in the cell and fisted the air in a victory salute. He ran out of the jail door and gulped with incomprehension and then fear as he saw Ranger Jones rising from the mud, his Texas Paterson in his fist. Schwarz tried to back away, but his boots slipped on the muddy boards of the sidewalk and the next he knew was the Ranger's bullet ploughing into him with the kick of twenty mules. He was sent flying back into the jailhouse to land on the floor. The men in the cell gawped at him as blood oozed from the hole in his chest. 'Fellas,' he gasped. 'Help me. Do something.'

'Sorry, pal,' Sheriff Polanski grinned. 'You got the keys. We're locked in. You're just gonna have to bleed to death.'

Out in the street, Cal Jones was covered in mud, looking like a corpse rising from the grave as he struggled to his feet. He turned towards the saloon, calling out, 'I've come to get you, Houck. You'd better crawl out from that stone you're hiding under like the sneaking monster you are. Come on out, you ain't scared of me, are you?'

Suddenly the sizzling electrified maw of the

storm boiled down upon them and thunder shook
the town to its foundations. Jake Houck slid from
under the saloon doors, lying on his belly, taking
aim at the Ranger with both guns. Fear and
hatred burned in his piggy little eyes. Who was
this mud-covered creature that bullets could not
harm? He emptied both pistols as Jones staggered
back from the impact. When all was still, Cal
swung back his fur jacket to reveal the ancient
Spanish breastplate he was wearing, now dented
by numerous bullet marks, and grimly smiled,
'Howja like the armour, Houck?'

Maybe he should have let him surrender, but he
had had enough. He raised the Paterson and
clapped out a shot. Houck's bare skull exploded
like a cantaloupe melon. Cal sighed. It was a
distasteful task.

'Look out!' Margarita screamed. 'It's Tonio.'

Tonio Cortez had, indeed, struggled from his
ropes, found a rifle overlooked by Margarita in his
saddle boot and had ridden hard and fast enough
through the storm, first to Riba and then on to
Duppa Springs. There he was in his black hat and
black clothes, sitting his horse at the far end of
the street, his rifle hugged into his shoulder. He
was taking aim at the Texan. He was well out of
range of Cal's revolver, and the Ranger wasn't
sure he had a slug left, anyhow. He stood bogged
in the mud, hardly able to move, awaiting his fate.

You never hear the sound of the bullet that kills
you, he thought, for some reason. The cord holding

his breastplate had been cut by a slug of Houck's that had grazed his shoulder. It had fallen away, leaving him exposed. But, it wasn't true. He *had* heard the clap of the rifle through the thunder. The bullet snarled past several feet away to his right. Either Tonio was a hell of a bad shot – or—

'Agh!' Cal heard the cry and turned to see Jimmy Ramirez tumbled from the sidewalk of the gunshop by Tonio's shot. But Ramirez was grovelling about in the mud and up on his knees raising a double-edged knife in his fist to hurl with his dying strength at the Texan. Cal pulled the Paterson trigger but there was an empty click. He had spent his last slug.

Tonio's rifle barked again and Ramirez hurtled back, sinking into the ooze. The knife whistled harmlessly past Cal's ear. 'Phew!' he whispered. 'Some of these guys just don't know when they're beat.'

Tonio brought his mustang rambling up through the mud. 'You oughta take better care. He nearly gotcha, pal.'

'I thought you were on their side?'

'Aw, any man can make a mistake. Killin' ain't much of a livin', is it?'

Cal glanced up at him and struggled through the knee-high mud and pouring rain to reach Margarita. He pulled his knife and cut her ropes, and supported her as she fell forward, sobbing and clinging to him. 'You're OK,' he soothed, stroking her hair, picking her up and carrying her over to the saloon. She was shivering and shuddering as he sat her down on a chair. 'Don't worry, you'll be fine.'

'It's been like a nightmare,' she whispered, as Tonio put a glass of rum in her hands.

'Sip that,' Cal urged. 'It will warm you.'

She did so and gradually ceased shuddering, trying to force a smile. 'Oh, Cal, it's like a miracle that you're still alive. I prayed and prayed. Perhaps God—'

'Yeah, perhaps He did help out. An' perhaps the ghost of that conquistador, too. That was a lucky find. Whoo! My chest! When them bullets hit me I thought I was a goner, I thought I was gonna have a heart attack. It's great to be back in the land of the living, ain't it?'

Margarita grimaced at the rum, but sipped some more, looking up at Tonio. 'What gave *you* a change of heart?'

'Aw,' Tonio flashed his conceited smile. 'JayCee reckons he's an OK guy. So do I.' He glanced, guiltily, at the girl. 'I'm sorry about back at the ranch.'

'Dad? Where is he? Is he all right?'

'They shot him. He's smashed up pretty bad. But I think he'll survive. He's a pretty tough old bastard.'

He took a slug of the rum and, when he turned back from the bar, Margarita was in Cal's muddy arms blissfully mid-kiss. Tonio grinned, headed for the door. 'Two's company. three's a crowd. I better go see what's happened to the sheriff. I guess we'll soon be hearing the sound of wedding bells.'

'Yeah,' Cal murmured, as he kissed her some more. 'You can bet on that.'

Twelve

JayCee Lanchester sat up in bed. The bullet had been cut from his chest and after uncertain days of drifting between the feverish realms of life and death he had pulled through. A poultice was bandaged across the wound, and his left leg was set in a cast of solid clay. 'So you've still got the gall to come here and ask for my daughter's hand in marriage, have you?' he snapped out, eyeing the Texan and Margarita. 'Well, in this county a gal has to be twenty-one before she can marry without her father's permission, and I ain't giving it.'

'If you don't give it,' Margarita burst out, angrily tossing her black hair, 'we'll go over to Apache County where a girl only has to be sixteen.'

'Ah, I see, the Ranger's turned you into a regular li'l rebel, has he?'

Cal stood, his thumbs in the pockets of his jeans, Margarita holding onto the crook of his arm. 'If you think it's your money I'm after, JayCee, think again. There's five thousand dollars reward cash on the Houck gang coming to me. I got my eye on a piece of land on the far side of the Mogollons, nice li'l ranch house, own water, good grazing.'

'I'm going with him, JayCee. You can't stop me. I'm going to learn to cook, and ride, and all the things you never let me do.'

'You know how much work there is for a woman running a smallholding? It ain't just the cooking, the sewing, the mending, the breadmaking, fire-lighting, wood-chopping, water-fetching, the baby-rearing, and so forth, it's the getting up 'fore dawn to milk the goats, feed the hogs, collect the eggs, that's before you git round to doing the weekly wash. You'll work your fingers to the bone. I ain't brought you up for that. You're a lady.'

'We can get some help in the house,' Cal said.

'I can do it,' Margarita insisted. 'I'm not help-less.'

'Hang on a minute, don't git on your high horse,' JayCee grinned. 'What you didn't wait for me to say was that I would give my permission only on two conditions: one, that you and this stubborn Texan, or Welshman, or whatever he is, accept as your dowry half my land stretching west from Tonto Creek to the Rio Verde, that's most of Pleasant Valley. And, two, you run cows on it, mostly, but I ain't objecting to a few sheep, as long as you keep 'em away from my land. Oh, and a third condition, I get over to have dinner with you now and again.'

'Dad!' Tears glimmered in Margarita's eyes as she threw herself upon JayCee and hugged his neck, kissing his cheek. 'You dark old lizard! Why couldn't you just come out and say it straight away? You – I love you.'

'Hey, hey,' he cackled, patting her hair. 'What's all this? I ain't known none of this in a long while. Ouch! You better git off my chest or I'll have a relapse.'

Lanchester stuck his hand out to Cal. 'Come on, boy, shake! I admit I was wrong about you. You're gonna accept this gift, aincha? I got to leave my land to somebody and I'd rather it went to a man I trust.'

Cal smiled and shook his hand firmly. 'I accept, JayCee. I'll do my best to look after your land and your gal.'

'The land's yours now, Cal, and so's the gal. Hey, git the bourbon outta the cupboard. Let's celebrate.'

And celebrate they did two weeks later when folks arrived from far and wide for the wedding and reception of Cal Jones and Margarita Lanchester. They drove their buggies and rode their horses across the lush grasslands now, after the rains, spangled with a myriad flowers, and through the canyons of cactus which were exquisitely in bloom attended by frantic hummingbirds sucking nectar. Out in front of the house there was an ox roasting and, symbolically, a sheep, too. Folks were surprised how tasty mutton could be. Long benches and tables, set up for the ranch hands, farmers, grooms, *vaqueros*, and Mexican maids, groaned under the weight of tortillas, enchiladas, pies and sweet potatoes, with salads from the kitchen garden, and dishes piled with pomegranates, peaches, strawberries and apricots, plus ice cream made with ice from the ranch ice-house and to wash it down an earthy red wine from California, or a Chardonnay for those who preferred the sparkle. Whatever, everybody was agreed it was the best wedding feast of them all.

The more important guests were fêted inside the ranch house at the banqueting table, for the governor of the territory, the general commanding the department, and other bigwigs were there. JayCee was back on his feet, albeit with crutches, and would walk with a limp from hereon. He sat on a raised platform at the head of the table beside Margarita, who was looking a picture in her mother's white lace over satin wedding dress, a flower-decked mantilla and veil. Cal looked a tad uncomfortable in a suit of grey homespun, and loose bowtie. When it came to the speeches everybody crowded in to stand around the table to listen and raise their glasses.

'Waal,' JayCee said, getting up on his crutches. 'I never thought in a month of Sundays my daughter would be marrying a dang-blatted sheepherder.'

He waited for the laughter to cease and added,

'Seriously, ladies and gen'lmen, this is a proud day
for me and one I wish my wife, Olivia' – he doffed
a hand at the big portrait of her and paused a few
seconds struggling to restrain tears – 'I wish she
might have seen. But, maybe, she's with us, too.
She would have been equally proud that today
Margarita has got hitched to a man who fought
with distinction in the Texas Rangers, who
showed his mettle in recent events, showed what
he's made of, one of the most decent, upstanding
young fellas it's been my privilege to meet – Cal
Jones.'

When the wild cheers and applause began to
die down, JayCee Lanchester went on, 'We all
know the cattle versus sheep wars have been
going on throughout the West for years now, and
we in the Tonto Basin have been as ferocious on
our side as most. Men have died and stock
destroyed. OK, I admit I fought against sheepmen
most my adult life, ran 'em off, same as many of
you here did, too. But Captain Cal Jones has
taught me another lesson. He has shown me that
we were in error. Sheep do not devastate the land,
nor leave a stench cattle will not tolerate, as
charged. There's good profit in sheep and my
advice to you ranchers is to start raising both.'

When many of the company began to demur,
JayCee called a hush. 'Hark! You hear that
gunfire? That's them Ticehursts and Tilburys up
in the hills still fightin' and feudin'! Do we want
to go on like them? No, of course we don't. So,

here's the toast to the new generation, Cal and Margarita, to show us the true way.'

After the wine had gone down and other toasts made, JayCee got to his feet again. 'There's one last toast. To Tonio, my son, yes, my son, and to his betrothed, Marietta, who, I guess you all know, was a *fille de joie*, as the Frenchies say, but who he intends to rescue from a life of sin. To him I'm giving my saloon, the Red Rays, in Riba. I'm sure his ma-in-law will help him make it a success.'

Tonio looked astonished. 'Hail,' he said, 'I don't know what to say. You calling me son, JayCee, after all this time, and this generosity . . . a saloon is what I've always wanted. You ain't drunk, are ya?'

'Nope, I figure a saloon's your natural element,' JayCee said, and grinned. 'My one regret is I'll lose my private booth.'

'It'll be kept for you, JayCee,' Tonio said. 'Or maybe I should say, Dad, though that's a bit of a tongue-twister for me.'

Outside, as the sun sank into a bed of dark clouds that promised more rain, the dancing had begun, but the old antagonisms were even reflected in the caller's song:

'First lady to the right,
Swing the man who shot the sheep. . . .'

A big farmer was whooping and swinging his

lardy lady around like a bag of meal, bouncing the boards, as the others whooped and clapped, a fine fury imbuing the whole affair, Westerners doing what they loved to do best, work hard and play harder. And Cal and Margarita swirled in each other's arms and clapped with the best of them.

When the leather-lunged caller had to go and take a breather Cal stepped up and yelled, 'Carry on dancin' y'all. I'll show ya how we do it in Texas.'

When the folks regrouped he sang out in his deep Welsh voice:

> *'Hark ye partners, rights the same,*
> *First lady to the left and do it again. . . .'*

He grinned at Sheriff Polanski, who was sat in the centre of the band, twanging his banjo and beaming at him.

JayCee Lanchester hopped up on his crutches beside his daughter. 'You know,' he said, as she smiled at him, 'I think you're going to have quite a time with this fella.'

X